HERCULES

THE DIARY OF A (SORT OF) HERO

Other books by Tom Vaughan

Bin Boy

A Gangster Stole My Trunks

HERCULES

THE DIARY OF A (SORT OF) HERO

TOM VAUGHAN

ILLUSTRATED BY

DAVID O'CONNELL

■SCHOLASTIC

Published in the UK by Scholastic, 2024
1 London Bridge, London, SE1 9BG
Scholastic Ireland, 89E Lagan Road, Dublin Industrial Estate,
Glasnevin, Dublin, D11 HP5F

SCHOLASTIC and associated logos are trademarks and/or
registered trademarks of Scholastic Inc.

Text © Tom Vaughan, 2024
Illustrations © David O'Connell, 2024

The right of Tom Vaughan to be identified
as the author of this work has been asserted by them under
the Copyright, Designs and Patents Act 1988.

ISBN 978 0702 32463 5

A CIP catalogue record for this book
is available from the British Library.

Printed and bound in Great Britain by Clays Ltd, Elcograf S.p.A
Paper made from wood grown in sustainable forests
and other controlled sources.

MIX
Paper | Supporting
responsible forestry
FSC® C018072

3 5 7 9 10 8 6 4 2

www.scholastic.co.uk

To Albie & Agatha

FRIDAY
1 SEPTEMBER

Hello. My name is **Hercules Braver** and this is my diary, which is going to document my start of secondary school.

Before we go any further, I should get the elephant out of the room. Yes, my name really is **Hercules**. Yes, I **know** that I am named after a super-strong, super-cool Greek hero.

Most people would **hate** having a name like Hercules. But I **love** it. Me and Other Hercules have **loads** in common.

I know this thanks to my best friend Pav. He knows **everything** there is to know about Greek gods and heroes and is always banging on about them. Pav's dad is Professor of Something-or-other at the University of Something-or-other and **loves** Greek myths. I think it's why Pav is always so on edge – because every night he's hearing bedtime stories of people being punished for all eternity. The Greek gods could be pretty harsh. For example, this one king chopped down the wrong tree to make a dining table. So, to punish him, the gods made him really, really, really hungry – so hungry that he ate himself.

Pass the ketchup, will you?

If that had happened to me, I'd just have gone to an all-you-can-eat buffet. My other best friend, Hatty, says they can't throw you out no matter how many times you go back for more.

Pav **loves** to tell me all about the Greek gods and heroes and draw family trees of them for me. It's pretty complicated. And most of the time I just pretend to listen. I'm only really interested in Hercules, as he is the cool one. Like I said, we have loads in common.

1) We're both **awesome**. For example, Other Hercules saved the world from these angry giants who wanted to kill the gods and rule over humankind. While, recently, I saved an old person who had been run over by a car. It was only a remote-controlled one, but she was still very grateful.

2) We're both **famous**. Hercules was the biggest

celebrity in Ancient Greece, and I've been on TV.
I was on the local news for getting stuck inside
a vending machine.

The hungry schoolchild says he climbed inside to retrieve a tube of Rolos.

SNACKS

Artist's impression of vending machine incident

People on the street still recognize me because of it.

3) We both have **three parents**. Hercules had
his birth dad, Zeus (King of the Gods), his birth

mum, Alcmene, and his stepdad, Amphitryon.
I've got Mum, my birth dad who I've never met
who lives in Greece, and my stepdad, Ken, who
brought me up.

However, Ken and Zeus couldn't be more different.

Ken is a physics teacher and likes tandem bikes, fishing
and inventing weird things, which is about as far away as you
can get from a lightning-bolt-throwing, thunderstorm-riding
king of the gods like Zeus.

Definitely not an
immortal god

Ken works as a teacher at my new school where I'm starting next week.

The first day of secondary school is without **question** the most important moment in your life. It's when reputations are made - when cool guys are forged and losers decided on. A kid at a bus stop once told me that.

The thing is, I'm worried that Ken is going to cramp my cools. But I've got **big** plans for how to make an impression on my first day.

Everyone is going to remember the name **Hercules Braver**. Mark my words.

SATURDAY
2 SEPTEMBER

Big school starts in two days. And I've **got** to be ready. I'm confident that I'm going to make **hundreds** of new friends. Actually, make that **thousands**.

However, I'm not so sure about Pav and Hatty. Especially Pav. He has none of my natural cools. For example: I've got a purple belt in karate (the coolest martial art). He has a black belt in chess (the nerdiest board game). At least he *would* have if chess teachers handed out belts. But they don't. I'm not sure what they hand out. Socks, maybe. Pav has lots of black socks.

chess socks

Hatty *might* make friends at big school. Or she might not. You never know with her. She could turn up acting cooler than a penguin in a freezer. Or she could turn up wearing her pyjamas and walking her pet rock, Rocky III.

Rocky III (Rocky I fell in a river.
Rocky II rolled off a cliff.)

So I have a plan to help them and to make sure everyone knows how **awesome** we are.

The Plan

Make sure everyone thinks we're the coolest new kids in school.

I unveiled The Plan to them this afternoon.

Pav, as usual, decided to suck the fun out of things. "Are you doing this because we had no friends in primary school after you cried on TV inside that vending machine?"

"I didn't cry!" I replied, shocked at how badly he'd misremembered it. "I was having a great time." Then I added: "But it *was* hot in there. My eyes *might* have been sweating a little bit."

"You had a snot bubble and were calling for your mummy,"

he replied. Then he paused and added under his breath: "And you peed your pants."

Obviously that didn't happen. "I've told you a **thousand** times, Pav," I said. "It was really, **really** hot! My legs were sweating!"

Hatty pulled a piece of paper from her backpack. It was a photo of me inside the vending machine. "It doesn't look like sweat."

sweating eyes

sweating leg

Actual photo

I stared at it. "Why do you have this in your backpack, Hatty?"

She shrugged. "I carry it around in case I need cheering up. If I'm scared or sad, I look at it and think: well, I'm not **nearly** as scared and sad as you were, so things could always be worse."

I dropped the photo on the floor and folded my arms. "I'm starting to think you're not even interested in The Plan."

"I am!" chimed Hatty. "I don't want us to be the unpopular kids any more."

"Good!" I said and unveiled the rest of it. "Because we're **definitely** not going to be! This Plan is going to show everyone how cool we *really* are."

The Plan

Make sure everyone thinks we're the
coolest new kids in school.
Dress cool
Act cool
Hand out business cards

It was brilliant in its simplicity. No further questions needed. Or so I thought.

"How do we dress cool if we have to wear a school uniform?" asked Pav.

"Hats!" replied Hatty confidently. "Hats and sunglasses!"

Hatty might be a bit odd, but sometimes she has great ideas. And I had *just* the accessory in mind.

Pav squirmed. "How, then, do we *act* cool?"

That one's obvious: I just need to be myself.

Hatty had a different take. "Simple, Pav: just *don't* be yourself."

She laughed, and Pav looked cross. Then he frowned even harder and said, "Point three is a rubbish idea."

"Yeah. I'm not so sure on that one," said Hatty. "We're starting a new school, not attending an IT conference."

Some people just can't see a brilliant idea when it is staring them in the face. Every big shot in the world has a business card. At least, they do on *The Apprentice*.

"What is the one **guaranteed** way to make sure everyone knows our names?" I asked.

They both opened their mouths to answer but I didn't let them.

"**Business cards!**" I cried. "And if they forget" - unlikely in my case, but maybe not in Pav's - "then they've got it written on a piece of card."

Dream business card

"Do you *really* think it's a good idea to draw so much attention to ourselves?" asked Pav, with his usual negative energy.

I rolled my eyes. "Attention is a **good thing**, Pav. Do you think Elon Musk would be famous if he didn't demand all that attention?"

And he didn't have a reply to that.

SUNDAY
3 SEPTEMBER

My stepdad, Ken, would **not** have been one of the cool kids at school. He **loves** school, he **loves** teaching and he **loves** science. He even does it in his free time – making weird inventions in our spare bedroom. I've always helped out because I thought we might invent something cool.

But I've recently realized that we are never going to build a robot or space rocket or self-playing electric guitar.

He's currently on the lookout for something to invent for the school science fair in October. He found me in my bedroom counting out the change from my piggy bank because I need £11 for my business cards.

"That looks like it's going to take ages," he said, sitting on the floor and helping me sort coins into piles. And then his eyes lit up. "Maybe we should invent a machine to do it! We could make it a project for the science fair."

"Yeah. Maybe," I said, although I'm pretty sure they already have those in banks.

He carried on helping me sort coins. "Are you excited to start secondary school?"

"Yeah!" I said, imagining everyone dribbling over my business cards.

That made him happy. "I was excited to go to school and learn stuff too!"

Not quite what I was getting at, but I let it slide.

He paused for a moment. I knew what this meant - he was gearing up to say something deep and meaningful.

"Herc, we both know I'm not your real dad..." he started to say.

I mean, he kind of *is* my real dad, because he's brought me up. But I know what he means - he's not my birth dad.

Ken continued, "But watching you grow up has been amazing. You're getting so big."

Really? I thought, excitedly looking down at my muscles.

"It seems like just yesterday that you were our little Herky-Werky." (That's the nickname he's always given me which I secretly **hate** because it makes me sound like a weird baby.)

He carried on. "Secondary school can be hard. Especially when you're suddenly a little fish in a big pond. I always ask the kids in my tutor group: what's more important than being popular?" He looked at me like he expected me to answer.

"Erm, **nothing**?"

"*Being yourself,*" he said. "That's the most important thing in the world."

That didn't make any sense. How could I be anyone *other* than myself? Unless I had a face transplant. And even then, my insides would still be me. Besides, he was wrong: everyone knows being popular is the **most** important thing in the world. If I was popular, I would have **no** problems! I'd have thousands of friends to say nice things about me, I'd get picked for any sports team I wanted, everyone would laugh at my jokes and I'd have a warm, fuzzy feeling inside the whole time (I imagine). So I just smiled and said, "OK."

"I'm looking forward to walking you in on your first day," Ken said. "Just like I did at nursery and primary school. Or you can ride on the back of the bike if you want?"

I fought to keep the smile on my lips because that wasn't part of **The Plan**. In fact, I was certain it would ruin it completely.

"Sure. I mean … maybe," I replied. And then I looked down and quickly carried on sorting coins.

I spent all my life savings (£5.86) on business cards. Mum thinks I'm ridiculous.

You're crackers.

But I told her I'm investing in my future and that

Pffffff. Details, details.

£5.86 will buy me **thousands** of friends. She said that's impossible as there aren't thousands of kids at the school.

I also picked out the **coolest** hat I own. Perhaps the coolest hat any eleven-year-old kid owns.

It's a beanie I saw in a snowboarding magazine. Actually, it's a copy of a beanie I saw in a snowboarding magazine that my aunt knitted for me. But it is **so cool** it's practically frozen.

Mega-cool hat

Mum saw me slip it in my backpack with my sunglasses and business cards. "Herc, you're not going to make a scene at school tomorrow, are you?" she asked carefully.

"Not at all," I replied. (Unless of course the scene was: new boy wins a thousand new friends in two minutes.)

She gave me a hug then and said, "All I've ever wanted is for you to be happy."

"Thanks," I replied. "It's all I've ever wanted as well." Then I added, "And for Pav to be less grumpy."

After that, there was just one more thing to do, and I

wasn't looking forward to it.

I found Ken sorting out his pencil case for the morning. I couldn't leave it any longer.

"Tomorrow, I think I'm going to walk in with Hatty and Pav."

Ken looked up at me. I could see immediately that he was surprised. "You don't want to come in on the back of my bike?" he asked. "It'll be … quicker."

It might be quicker, but there was no way I was going to win thousands of new friends by turning up on the back of a tandem bike … ridden by the physics teacher.

"It's OK," I replied. "Pav, erm, needs some moral support."

He looked a little sad, but he did a good job of hiding it.

"No worries at all," he said, then smiled. "You're getting so grown up now – of course you want to arrive with your friends. I guess I'll see you in school, Herky-Werky! You can come see my physics lab?"

"Um, sure. If I'm not too busy on my first day," I said.

Busy making **thousands** of new friends, that is. Anyway, I'd better stop writing and go to sleep. I need all my energy tomorrow for what is going to be the **greatest day of my life.**

MONDAY
4 SEPTEMBER

Today is the first day of **Big School** - possibly the most **important day of my life**. I spent all last night dreaming about The Plan.

Pav, Hatty and I met at the end of our road. Ken and Mum waved me off from our front garden.

Ken said he wasn't actually crying and that he had just cut an onion. But it's unlikely as he had Weetabix for breakfast.

On the way in, I could tell Pav was nervous because he was babbling about Greek myths (which he does when he's on edge).

He was telling me all about Other Hercules's twelve labours.

And then Hatty started talking over him and telling us all about our new school and the weird things she'd found out about it from her big brother in Year Ten. For example, one kid kept a canteen fish finger in his locker and it didn't go mouldy for eight months. Also, there is a **monster** that lives in the school pond.

But I wasn't really listening to her *either* because my mind was focused on one thing and one thing only:

The Plan.

Actually, my mind was focused on two things and two things only: **The Plan** and a really annoying fly that wouldn't leave me alone.

Everything was in place for The Plan. We'd all found hats and sunglasses and I had my business cards. (Pav and Hatty claimed they'd forgotten to buy theirs.)

I stopped one minute before we reached the school gates, by a fence separating us from what seemed to be a very filthy school pond. I wanted to mark the moment with a speech.

"Hatty, Pav: you've been my best friends since we were six."

"Thanks." Hatty beamed.

"Also your only friends," mumbled Pav.

I held my palm out to shut him up.

"When we walk through those gates, life as we know it is going to change. We are going to become the legends we were born to be. We will make **thousands** of new friends..."

"Maybe even **millions**..." added Hatty.

I thought for a second, then decided she was right. "Maybe even **millions**." Pav scowled but I continued. "But, whatever happens, you two will still be my best friends."

Pav's face softened. Hatty hugged me.

Then I stood tall. "So, are we ready for **The Plan**?"

"**Ready!**" replied Hatty.

"Not ready," mumbled Pav.

On the count of three, we put on our hats and sunglasses.

They both stared at my hat.

"Um, Herc…?" said Hatty. "What is *that*?"

"It's a ski beanie," I replied.

"It looks like a giant poo," said Pav.

"Well … it's not a poo," I snapped back. "It's fashion."

The annoying fly began circling around my head even faster. I swatted it away. "Let's go!"

We turned the corner and I could hear the noise of kids in the playground – our future friends. I took a deep breath. Then, together, we stepped through the school gates.

In front of us was a sea of kids. They were all in the same grey uniform, and all much bigger than us. The school behind them was a long, flat rectangle made of grey and glass. It seemed bigger than it had when I'd looked around. This was easily twenty times the size of our primary school. A kid could easily become invisible in a place like this. Unless, of course, they had a Plan.

A Plan that was already working perfectly because everybody was turning to look at us.

"Isn't that the kid who peed his pants inside a vending machine?" asked someone.

"Why's he wearing a *poo* on his head?" laughed someone else.

"It's a ski beanie," I said, but they were laughing so didn't seem to hear.

Pav leaned into my ear and mumbled nervously, "Everyone's looking and laughing at us."

"Exactly!" I whispered. "We have their attention!" Now it was time to make the most of it and bring out the big guns. Or rather, the small cards.

Hercules Braver.
Cool kid.

New business card (couldn't
afford my dream version)

I offered one to the nearest kid. But she just stared at my head and giggled, "There's a fly trying to land on your poo hat."

"It's a ski beanie," I corrected her, and offered a business card to two cool-looking kids, one of whom was holding a football.

They were exactly the kind of awesome new friends we needed. But all they did was point at my hat.

Why did **no one** want my business cards?

A tiny kid with curls started waving his hand. "Can I have one?" he pleaded.

He wasn't exactly the kind of image we were going for. But I handed him one anyway.

"Woooooow," he said as if it was the most amazing thing he'd ever owned.

"Anyone else?" I shouted. But I couldn't hear the replies over the sound of laughter.

Hatty leaned in again. "Herc, I think I'm going to take my hat off."

Suddenly, a shadow blotted out the sun. The ground started to shake (I think), and the sea of sniggering faces began to part. Then, from amongst the crowd, emerged a giant.

Or at least he looked like a giant.
I think he was a Year Ten.

He had a nasty smirk on his face.

"Look what we have here. Some attention-seeking newbies. Why are you wearing a poo on your head? Couldn't attract enough flies with your fart smell?"

The annoying fly landed on my cheek. I swatted it away and sighed. Maybe he didn't hear me before? I raised my voice and spoke extra clearly: "It's - a - ski beanie!"

Everyone sucked in air like I shouldn't have said that.

There was a moment of silence, then... "Who the hell do you think you are, talking to **me** like that?" the giant said.

Finally! Someone wanted to know my name!

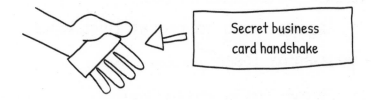

Secret business card handshake

Now was the moment to bring out my **ace card**.

"What are you doing?" asked the giant.

"Offering you a handshake."

Slowly, warily, he took my hand and then...

OOOOOWWWWWWWARRGHHHHHHHH!!!!!!

He dropped it and a bloodied business card fell to the floor.

"You've given me a paper cut!!" He gripped his finger, blood seeping out of a tiny cut.

Next to me, Pav's head had practically retreated into his shoulders.

Hatty whispered in my ear, "He looks angry, Herc." She was right. The giant looked furious.

"You're going to regret this! What's your name, loser?" he cried.

"Hercules," I replied. "Hercules Braver."

"Hercules Braver?" he sneered. "Who do you think you are, some sort of Greek hero?" Then he laughed a mean laugh and said, "You look more like a Greek yoghurt to me! Weak ... pale ... and unpopular!"

He looked really happy at his bad joke. And all his mates seemed to think it was the funniest thing ever.

Huh huh huh!

Nice one, Malky!

You're so funny, Malky!

Hatty leaned into my ear again. "I don't think this is going well."

I think she might have been right. Turns out making friends in Big School is harder than I thought. And it was about to get even harder...

Coo-ee!

Ken appeared, riding through the playground on his tandem bike and waving at me. "Want to come see the physics lab, Herky-Werky?"

I could feel my cheeks flush. Not *now*. I gave a weak wave as he disappeared around the corner. Then everyone laughed even harder.

"*Herky-Werky!*" hooted Malky as the fly landed in my ear. "I didn't realize you were *Mr Braver's* son. Now it all makes sense!"

The fly left my ear and landed on Malky's shoulder. That stupid insect had really ruined my first day at Big School.

It was payback time.

Without thinking, I lifted my hand and **HI-YA** - I landed a karate-chop *right* where the fly was. Which, I quickly realized, was right on Malky's shoulder.

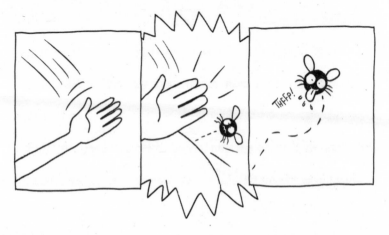

A scream exploded.

"OOOOWWWWWWARRGHHHHHHH!!!!!!"

It was mine.

That **really, really** hurt. I hopped up and down and clutched my throbbing hand.

Malky didn't look hurt. But he did look even angrier. He reached down and picked me up by the collar.

"Did you just *karate-chop* me?"

"I can explain," I said. But before I could, the crowd scattered, leaving just me, Pav, Hatty and Malky. An old man was marching towards us, and he looked even angrier than Malky.

"What is this?" he shouted. **"Fighting?** On the first day? You lot, in my office, **NOW!"**

As I feared: the old man was the headmaster, Mr Geras.

We had to wait outside his office while he lectured Malky. Pav was really cross with me. "Why did you have to draw all that attention to us?"

Mr Geras

"Relax," I said, nursing my hand. "People were probably impressed at how accomplished my karate skills are. I do have a purple belt."

"Yeah," said Hatty. "But you found it in a lost-property bin."

Pffff. Details. Details.

The door opened and Malky walked out, staring at me in RAGE. "I'm going to get you, *Herky-Werky*," he hissed.

Pav, Hatty and I filed into Mr Geras's office and stood in front of his desk while he lectured us. Behind him, a big ginger cat gave me a death stare from inside a cage.

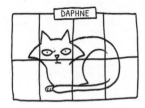

It was time to lay a charm offensive on Mr Geras. "What a well-fed cat you have, sir! Can I stroke it?"

"No, you cannot!" he snapped.

"Why's he in a cage, sir?" asked Hatty, while Pav went "*Shhhhhhhhh*" between gritted teeth.

"It's Daphne's safe space," Mr Geras said sharply. "She's a house cat so she can't go outside."

"It's unethical to have a cat who can't go outsi—"

"Silence!" shouted Mr Geras, cutting Hatty off. Then he

banged on about how first impressions are really, **really** important (like he needs to tell **me** that!) and how we weren't making a very good one. Then he said some other stuff too:

I tried my best to look impressive and likeable.

When he'd finished talking, he stared long and hard at us, like he was chewing over what he was going to do with us. Finally, he said:

"As a punishment, you can help out at Nature Club."

"What's that?" asked Hatty.

"It's a project to clean out the school pond."

"The one with the monster in it?" she asked.

Mr Geras glowered at her. "There is **no monster** in the school pond."

Which, of course, is **exactly** what you'd say if you had a monster in your pond and didn't want people to know about it.

I forced my smile even bigger. "I would be **delighted** to clean out your stinking pond, sir!"

There was a long silence. Mr Geras's wrinkly eyes inspected me. Finally, he said, **"Hercules Braver ...** I'm going to be watching you closely."

I flashed Pav and Hatty a thumbs up. But by the looks on their faces, they didn't seem to think that was a good thing.

In the evening, Ken iced my swollen hand. "You didn't come see the physics lab today," he said. "Maybe tomorrow?"

"Erm, yeah..." I replied.

Mum was angrily scribbling in her Organizer, a big black book that she puts everything in - diary dates, shopping lists, addresses. She put the pen down and sighed. "Did you really have to karate-chop a kid, Herc? On your first day?"

"It was an accident, Mum. I was karate-chopping a **fly**. And I know what I'm doing! I have a purple belt in karate."

"You found that in a lost-property bin!" she snapped. Then she let out a long breath and said, "What do you want to get out of secondary school, Hercules?"

I think it might have been one of those trick questions to make me think about things seriously, which I did.

"The usual. To be worshipped and adored."

She folded her arms tighter and muttered, "Just like your father." By which I think she meant my birth father, who she *never* usually mentions.

"Look, Mum," I said, trying to make her see sense, "*you* gave me this **awesome** name. I've got to live up to it. No one called Hercules has **ever** been a loser."

Mum's expression softened for a moment, and she reached out to touch my shoulder. "You'll never be a loser, Herc. And that name was **not** my choice. It was your birth dad's. He said you had to have a 'rockstar' name, just like him." She made little quotation marks with her fingers around the word "rockstar". "But you don't have to prove yourself to anybody."

"Exactly. You're brilliant as you are," said Ken, but I wasn't listening.

"A *rockstar* name?"

"Yes."

"Just like my birth dad?"

"Yes."

"Is he famous? Is he a rockstar?"

Mum thought long and hard, then finally she said, "In a manner of speaking. But you're nothing like him, Herc, and that's no bad thing. Being famous doesn't make you a good or trustworthy person. It makes you..."

41

But I'd stopped listening completely because my head was spinning with the news that my birth dad is a rockstar. How cool is that?

TUESDAY
5 SEPTEMBER

I bowled up for Day 2 of Big School ready to **crush it**. If I was the son of a rockstar (in a manner of speaking), then I **totally deserved** to be mega popular. Day 1 might not have gone as well as I'd hoped, but today was a **fresh start**.

I strode into the playground with Hatty and Pav, giving it some rockstar swagger. Immediately, a Year Ten must have noticed, as he took one look at me and came over.

"**Hercules Braver**, rockstar's son," I said, offering my hand.

He didn't take it. Instead, he leaned in and sniffed my head. I *had* been using particularly minty shampoo, I thought, but this was *still* weird.

And that's when he shouted across the playground to

Malky: "*Still* smells of **poo**!" And then everyone laughed like it was the funniest thing in the world.

Hatty sucked her breath in. "Ouch."

Things didn't get any better from there. About ten other people mentioned my "poo hat" or "poo head", like they'd never seen a snowboarding magazine. And even my form teacher seems to think I'm a troublemaker for accidentally getting into a fight with Malky.

So now I'm writing this on the toilet during lunch, waiting for Malky and his mates to leave the dining hall so I can eat something. So far, Day 2 hasn't gone any better than Day 1. I **desperately** need to get The Plan back on track. I'll do **anything** to convince people just how great I really am.

After school, we had our first Nature Club. A small kid with curls was waiting for us by the pond.

"Hi, I'm Hercules," I said, eying up the revolting pond.

"We've met before!" he said.

I looked him up and down. He must have me confused with another awesome cool kid. "No, we haven't."

"Yes! We have!"

"I have a photographic memory for faces," I replied.

He pulled out my business card.

"Hmmmm," I said, raising an eyebrow. "Where did you get this?"

"You gave it to me on our first day."

I stared long and hard at his face. Nothing was coming back to me.

"I'm Natthew," he said.

"*Natthew?*"

"Natthew," he confirmed. Which is a weird name.

"Have you been sent here by Mr Geras as well, Matthew?" asked Pav, getting his name wrong, because he one hundred per cent said Natthew.

"I just like to volunteer for stuff," he said. "Plus, I saw

that you were signed up for Nature Club, Hercules, and I thought we could be friends?"

I forced a smile and said nothing. Poor guy – you could smell the desperation on him.

"Hope you don't mind fighting a **pond monster**, Matthew!" interjected Hatty, also getting his name wrong.

The smile fell from his face. "A *monster*?"

"Yeah!" said Hatty. "It eats birds. Sometimes even cats. Maybe even students. My brother swears on it."

"Relax, Matthew. There's no such thing as a pond monster," said Pav.

"Of course there is!" Hatty said. "Look around you. People are clearly scared to come near the pond – otherwise how did it get so filthy?"

"School funding cuts?" said Pav, but Hatty talked over him.

"Legend has it, a kid in the nineteen nineties lured it out of the pond one night with a Curly Wurly,

wrestled it and stole one of its teeth. He wore it on a necklace for the rest of his time at school. He's legendary."

"Legendary?" I asked, raising an eyebrow.

"Yup. People still talk about him now, all these years later."

Pav blew his cheeks out dismissively. But my brain was **fizzing** with possibilities. If I wrestled the pond monster and stole its tooth, I could become a legend. **No one** would remember my sweating legs or my snowboarding beanie.

And then an even bigger thought occurred to me - why did I have to stop at capturing a tooth? I took a step forward and put my hands on my hips.

"I, Hercules Braver, shall capture this pond monster, once and for all!"

Pav scowled. Hatty beamed. Natthew gave me a thumbs up. This was **definitely** the best idea I had ever had.

As Hatty, Pav and Natthew started trying to heave a rusty shopping trolley out of the mud, I tried to figure out how you go about catching a pond monster.

Annoyingly, the person among us who knew the most about monsters was also the least likely to help. Finally, I took a chance and said, "Pav, they were always killing monsters in Greek myths. How did they do it?"

Pav's fingers slipped on the shopping trolley, and it rolled back into the pond. He looked at me, torn – he clearly

48

didn't want anything to do with the pond monster, but he also **loved** talking about Greek myths.

Finally, he said, "Well, in one of Other Hercules's first labours, he killed a many-headed lake monster called the Hydra."

This got me excited. "How'd he do it?"

"He chopped its heads off with a flaming sword so they couldn't grow back."

Interesting.

"Where can we get one of those?" I asked. "Tesco?"

Pav's eyebrows lowered. "You can't get them on the high street."

"Then ... the internet!" exclaimed Hatty.

I huffed. "That'll take ages. I need to catch it as **soon** as I can."

"You could use a net?" offered Natthew. "Or a cage?"

There was a silence as we all looked at him.

Finally, I said, "Natthew, you might have a strange name ... but you could well be on to something." Because I knew **exactly** where we could find a cage.

Five minutes later, I was peeking into Mr Geras's empty office. Empty of **humans**, that is.

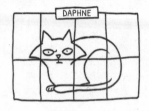

DAPHNE

50

I could definitely borrow that cage and have it back without Mr Geras ever noticing. *It'll be the purr-fect crime*, I thought, then LOLed at the brilliance of my own joke.

I opened the cage door and let the cat out. "Nice kitty." She purred and rubbed her neck on my hand. I gave her a little stroke, then tucked the empty cage under my arm. There was a jar of olives on Mr Geras's desk. I opened them up and gave one to Daphne. She gobbled it down and licked her lips. She obviously loves olives as much as I do. I popped one in my mouth and slurped on the salty juice. Yum!

I headed for the door, making sure not to let her out as I remembered that she is a house cat and can't go outside. As I slipped out into the cool of the hallway, I felt a pang of sympathy for the little thing. It was so stuffy in the office. On the spur of the moment, I went back in and opened the window, so she could get a bit of air. Sometimes I surprise myself how thoughtful I am.

Then I headed out the door with the cage, making sure to

close it behind me because I'd have **hated** for the cat to escape.

I stood by the pond with the cage. "Now what?"

"We need bait!" said Hatty. "Natthew?"

"Do you really think we should feed him to the..." I started to say.

"Here you go!" Natthew offered a Curly Wurly. On reflection, that was probably the simpler option.

After much discussion, we agreed that our monster-catching device would look like this:

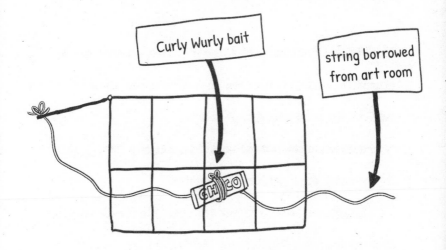

Curly Wurly bait

string borrowed from art room

"So," I recapped, "we throw the cage into the pond. Then, when the string starts tugging, it means the monster is eating the Curly Wurly... We pull the string hard, which will pull the door shut and trap the monster. Then we haul it out and boom, we have caught the pond monster and become immortal legends. Any questions?"

Natthew put his hand up. "Will I get my Curly Wurly back?"

"Probably not. Unless you cut it from the monster's stomach."

"Whose cage is it?" asked Pav.

"The headmaster's cat's. But it's fine – I shut her in his office. We can return the cage afterwards. Once we've subdued the pond monster, of course."

Pav tried to say something, but I spoke over him. "Right! Hatty, would you like to do the honours?"

"Yes, please!" Hatty heaved the cage into the air. We all counted down together (except for Pav).

"Three. Two. One."

Then she hurled the cage into the middle of the pond. It landed with an almighty splash, bobbed around in the water for a moment, and then began to sink beneath the surface. The trap was set.

"Who's holding the string?" I asked.

Pav, Hatty and Natthew all stared at me. "We thought you were?"

I spun around just in time to see it floating in the brown sludge at the other end of the pond.

"Get it!" I screamed.

We all ran for it, but Natthew tore ahead. He might have tiny legs, but he can move like a greased cheetah. He flew around the pond and lunged for the string, wading in up to his knees - but it slipped through his fingers and disappeared into the bog water.

"Well, I guess that's that," said Pav as I scrunched my face up in frustration.

"I still can't believe we let a pond monster slip through our fingers," I said to Pav and Hatty as we headed home through the car park. "Maybe we can try and get hold of a flaming sword?"

Pav stopped and let out a big angry sigh. "There's no such thing as a **flaming sword!** There's also no such thing as a **pond monster!** And we just got ourselves in **loads of trouble** by losing Mr Geras's cat cage!"

I put a hand on his shoulder. "Relax, buddy," I said. "It's not lost. We know exactly where it is: at the bottom of a pond. No one saw me take it, so he'll never know it was us.

And Daphne is locked up safely in his office. So there's really

nothing to worry about."

WEDNESDAY
6 SEPTEMBER

Mr Geras's cat is missing. And he is **livid**. Well, actually, he's half livid, half distraught.

At assembly, he gave a long, teary, angry speech. "Yesterday, someone **stole** my beloved Daphne from my office! Who would do such a thing?" (Cue blubbing.) "If I find out it was a student in **this school**..." (Cue rage.) "**I will come down on them like a tonne of bricks!**"

I was dreading seeing Pav at break. Because I knew he was going to say:

Are you certain you didn't let Daphne out of his office?

I pulled my best poker face.

Yup.

"You're lying! I **know** you're lying!"

"Fine," I whispered, pulling him to the corner of the playground by the bins so that no one could hear us. "I opened the window a crack just to let some air in because it was so stuffy and..."

Pav's face dropped. "Oh my word. She's an inside cat. She can't go outside. You've lost her. I can't believe you've lost her.

We're in so much trouble." Etc etc.

Pav always overreacts. "It's **fine**," I said. "We'll just get her back. How hard can it be to find a cat? We'll look in the cat pound. Or..." I thought where else a cat might hang out. "The cat hotel."

"There's no such thing as a cat hotel..." he said, but I wasn't listening as a thought had dropped into my head like a Mentos into a Coke bottle. Mr Geras had no idea it was us who lost Daphne. So that meant...

"When we find her, Mr Geras will think we're **heroes**!"

It was **SO** simple: capture the pond monster and find Daphne and the whole school, Mr Geras included, will think we are **absolute legends!** I was speechless with the brilliance of my vision. Pav was too. His mouth hung open, and he stared at me wordlessly.

But before he could shower me with praise, a shadow passed over us, blocking out the sun. It was Malky.

"Hanging out with the rest of the rubbish, I see," he snarled.

"Um..."

Before I could say anything, Malky leaned in, thrusting his bandaged finger into my face. "Don't think I've forgotten. I'm going to get you, *Herky-Werky*. Just you wait."

With that, he turned and left.

"You're shaking," I said to Pav.

"No, *you're* shaking," he replied, but he probably only thought that I was shaking because he was shaking so much. Because I **definitely** wasn't scared.

I looked around at the crowded playground and at all the kids eying us, sniggering at Pav shaking so much. This was **not** how I'd imagined secondary school would go. I thought I'd be a complete legend with millions of friends. Not hiding by the bins with a trembling Pav.

I needed to fix things. I needed friends to protect me from Malky. **Cool** friends.

And that was when I saw Natthew across the playground. Obviously he was no help, but he **was** talking to two cool kids I recognized from the first day. There was only one thought going through my head: if they like Natthew, they'll **definitely** like me cos I'm twenty times cooler!

I rushed over. "**Hi, guys!**"

Natthew replied. "Hi, Hercules!"

I was looking at the two cool kids, but they didn't say anything.

"Have you met Billy and Ben?" asked Natthew.

"**Hi!**" I said. But they just played it cool.

"What are we talking about?" I asked.

"We were just talking about Matthew's big brother," said Billy, getting Natthew's name wrong. "Apparently they've completed *Golden Deer Quest* together."

Golden Deer Quest is a computer game that everyone goes **wild** about. You have to travel across a mythical world fighting monsters in search of this golden-antlered deer. I've never got past level one, but that's because I've never tried that hard.

GOLDEN DEER
— QUEST —

"Yeah," said Natthew. "And he's going to buy me *Golden Deer Quest II* when it comes out in six weeks."

"Oh, nice one," said Billy. "Can't wait for that to drop."

"Does your brother go here?" I asked Natthew.

"He used to!" Natthew beamed.

"He holds the school one hundred metres record," said Ben. Being unbelievably fast obviously runs in Natthew's family.

"And he used to be in the school band," added Billy. "Now he's got his own record deal."

What? I can't believe Natthew's brother is that cool.

And then it dawned on me – he isn't the only person with a famous musician in the family.

I blurted out: "My dad is awesome too! He's a rockstar!"

Billy frowned. "I thought your dad was Mr Braver?"

"No!" I said, forcing out a big laugh. "He's my stepdad. I mean my birth dad. He lives in Greece."

"And he's a rockstar?" asked Ben.

"In a manner of speaking."

Billy raised his eyebrows. "Cool," he said.

"Yeah, let us know if he's in town," said Ben.

Then they split, leaving me standing there with Natthew, who was saying something, but I wasn't listening. I wasn't listening because my head was spinning with a brilliant thought... A thought so important I had to sneak off immediately and write all this down.

I have a new plan. Capturing the pond monster and finding Daphne are just the *appetizers* on my quest for awesomeness. Because, to become truly epic, I know exactly what I need to do:

I need to write to my rockstar dad and get him to visit me!

It's genius. I'm genius. It's probably the **best idea** I've ever had.

"That's the **worst** idea you've ever had." No prizes who said that. This guy

We were cleaning out the pond again after school for Nature Club. At least Hatty, Pav and Natthew were. I'd baited the bank with Curly Wurlys in the hope the pond monster would crawl out and I could overpower it with a Nerf gun.

"Even if he does come here, your dad's not going to magically make you popular," said Pav, scooping leaves out of the seemingly bottomless pond. "Besides, are you sure your mum won't mind you writing to him?"

I'd thought about this. "I'm not going to tell her." (Which is definitely the best solution as she doesn't like to talk about my birth dad. Although it does raise a big problem: how on earth am I going to find out his address?)

Pav's face dropped further. "*What?!* Are you being serious? You'll get in so much trouble. And ... you know he's probably not actually a rockstar, Herc?"

I'd pretty much had it up to the eyeballs with Pav's negative energy. "He is! In a manner of speaking. And he's going to come here and make us mega popular." I took a breath then added, "Anyway, do *you* have any ideas about how to make us cool?"

"What if you didn't try so hard?" Natthew piped up. "My dad said that if I just be myself, I'll make friends."

I put a hand on his shoulder. "Natthew, you're in dreamland. Coolness doesn't just *happen*. It's **created**," I replied. "Now shush, or you'll scare the pond monster away. I'll never catch it with all this jabbering."

And with that I trained my Nerf gun back on the pond and tried to figure out how I was going to find my birth dad's address.

THURSDAY
7 SEPTEMBER

I was so exhausted after the effort I spent at Nature Club that I fell asleep updating this diary last night. But to summarize: the pond monster is still at large, and I haven't yet worked out how I'm going to write to my birth dad.

What's more, Daphne still hasn't come back. But it's a good thing she's still missing - because when we find her, Mr Geras will think we're the greatest students he's **ever had**. Which can't come soon enough. Ever since my first day, Mr Geras seems **convinced** that I'm trouble. He's **always** watching us suspiciously from his window during break time.

Pav, Hatty, Natthew and I spent all of today's break looking for Daphne near the playing fields. At least, Pav, Natthew and I did. Hatty got bored and started scratching something on a tree with a sharp rock.

I wandered over and my eyes nearly popped. Carved into the tree were the words:

I snatched the rock off her. "We're already in enough trouble," I hissed.

She shrugged and as I glanced over to Mr Geras's window, my eyes locked with his. I dropped the rock like a hot potato and tried to look innocent. But it clearly didn't work, as five minutes later he was staring at the tree, turning dark red with anger and giving me death stares.

It also didn't help that we were also getting distracted constantly by Malky and his friends sniffing my head and saying it smells of poo, which they're wrong about because I washed it for longer last night just in case. It was **SO** annoying.

But not **nearly** as annoying as what I found stuck to the noticeboard as I was heading to class.

SCIENCE FAIR:
TUESDAY 17TH OCTOBER

Have you got what it takes to invent the coolest new gadget in town?

Compete against

AWESOME TEAM BRAVER

Mr Braver and super-cool junior inventor Hercules Braver for the annual Science Fair Invention Prize!

Great. Just great. How can I even hope to be awesome if Ken keeps embarrassing me?

For the rest of the day, people were whispering things like "*awesome team Braver*" and "*super-cool junior inventor*" and sniggering.

Then I heard someone mutter, "He should've invented some plastic trousers!"

But the person who said it is obviously not very clever because plastic trousers would have just made my legs even sweatier in that vending machine.

On the way home from school, Pav **kept** trying to convince me to ask my mum for permission before I write to my birth dad.

"But she'll just say no!" I replied.

"Then surely there's a **reason** she'd say that?"

I thought long and hard. "Is it that the stamps might be too expensive?"

Pav shook his head and huffed.

"Look, Pav," I went on, "I know in my heart that my

birth dad is absolutely awesome. Like ... think of the most awesome, most famous dad in the whole wide universe."

He looked at me sideways. "Zeus?"

"*Zeus?!*" I said. Why does Pav always have to bring it back to Greek myths?

"I mean, he's **King of the Gods** and he's had thousands of children, and lots of them became Greek gods and goddesses, as well as kings and queens."

I thought about it for a second. "I was thinking more along the lines of Dwayne Johnson." Pav looked away again. "Come on! Imagine if my dad was someone like The Rock! Everyone would think I was the **coolest kid** in school!"

"Well. Good luck finding Dwayne Johnson's address. It's not like it'll be in your mum's address book or something!" scoffed Pav.

Pav might have been making a rubbish joke, but he was right - that's **exactly** where my birth dad's address will be!

I've just pulled off one of the greatest heists of all time.

Yoink!

I'm in my bedroom with the Organizer now. My birth dad's address **has** to be in here somewhere...

OK, that was **much** harder than I thought it would be.

I leafed through it, looking for **any** addresses in Greece. But there was nothing. I went through it again, and again, and there was still **nothing.** That's when I threw it on the floor in despair and a little folded-up scrap of paper fell out. I opened it out and saw this written in faint pencil:

ZOOEY
OLYMPUS
ATHENS 157 71
GREECE

It has to be my birth dad's address!

I grabbed a piece of paper and furiously scribbled a letter.

Dear Zooey,

I am Hercules Braver and I am eleven years old. I like crisps and being awesome. I have a purple belt in karate, and I am so strong that I can lift a train. Just a toy one at the moment, but I'm building up to a real one. I think you might be my dad. Mum says you are an absolute **legend** and that you called me Hercules? I'd love to meet you. I have another dad called Ken – my stepdad – and he's really nice, but he isn't exactly cool, so it'd be great to see where I get my awesomeness from! You could come to my school and show everyone how cool you are, and everyone will think we are both complete **heroes**.

Best wishes,

Hercules (your son)

Then I read it over, before scribbling at the bottom:

P.S. This is a secret so don't tell Mum.

Now the letter is safe under my pillow. There's **no reason** Mum should ever know about it. I'm pretty brilliant at keeping secrets.

FRIDAY
8 SEPTEMBER

Today is the day we are going to find Mr Geras's cat for definite. How hard can it be to find a chubby ginger cat?

Heading off to school now. Next time I write in this, we'll probably be his **favourite** students. Maybe of **all time!**

Mr Geras really has it in for me. He jumped out on Hatty and me as we were heading to break.

"Did you scratch something on school property yesterday, Braver?"

"No, sir," I replied, throwing a secret scowl at Hatty.

"Why, sir, have you seen something?" asked Hatty, with a face as innocent as a baby rabbit. "What did it say? Was it *rude*?"

He went red again and his eye started to twitch. Finally, he said: "I'm **watching you**, Braver." Then he turned and left. I think the worry about his missing cat is really getting to him.

All of which made it even **more urgent** for us to find Daphne **ASAP**. Pav reckons she's wandered into a school building and got trapped. He said we need to do a full search of the campus. Hatty thinks that she just doesn't want to come back because she hates being an inside cat. She said that we should lure her into a cage trap like the one we made for the pond monster (except not underwater). The only problem is, Hatty doesn't have a cage or know how we can get one. So we're stuck with Pav's idea.

The search of the school grounds took **ages** and there was no sign of Daphne **anywhere**. Pav asked Natthew along, who was absolutely no help and just kept saying encouraging things but not **actually** finding the cat. Hatty made lots of purring noises and filled her pockets with tuna, which was really smelly and still didn't coax Daphne out.

Towards the end, Pav was getting pretty grumpy, so I tried to cheer him up by chatting about Greek myths. "Didn't Other Hercules once have to find a cat?"

"Yes, he did," replied Pav. "It was his second labour. He had to track down an animal called the Nemean Lion."

"What happened?"

"He found it, killed it and wore its fur as a cape," said Pav.

"Awesome!" replied Hatty.

Pav glanced at me. "Don't get any ideas."

"What? I wasn't!" I lied.

Although, on reflection, that would **not** impress Mr Geras.

By the time we reached the last building, the school gym, it was getting dark, and we were getting so hungry that Hatty started eating her pocket tuna.

I opened the equipment cupboard and called for Daphne with no luck. I turned to Pav, Natthew and Hatty. "I don't think the cat's trapped or scared. I think there is only one plausible explanation."

"What's that?" asked Pav.

"The pond monster ate Daphne."

Pav flapped his hands angrily. "How many times have I told you? There is **no pond monster!** Daphne has not been eaten. And if you hadn't let her out in the first place, we wouldn't be in this mess!"

Ugh. Not *that* again. "How many times do I have to tell *you*?" I replied. "It's a **brilliant** thing I lost that cat - when we find her and hand her back to Mr Geras, he is going to think we're **awesome!** And even though you are always grumpy,

I'll still share the glory with you."

Pav folded his arms and turned away. "Can we go home?" he said.

Just then, I heard a rustling up in the gallery above the squash courts.

"Did you hear that?" I asked. "That could be Daphne!"

It was practically pitch-black in the gym and we still hadn't found the light switch. I didn't want to go up there in the shadows on my own. I looked at Hatty first.

"Are you being serious?" she said, scooping loose tuna into her mouth with her fingers. "No way am I going up there. What if it's a ghost?"

I looked at Pav. He scowled.

I looked at Natthew. "I'll come with you," he offered. But if there *was* a ghost up there, no way did I want Natthew being all nice and making friends with it.

"Let's leave it," I said. "We can always come back tomorrow when it's light."

So we turned and left. But just as I was closing the door, I took one last glance at the gallery. I had the creepiest feeling someone was watching me from up there. But I couldn't see anything.

We walked home. Pav was still in a mood, so I tried to cheer him up. "Don't you **wish** you could just summon up Other Hercules to help?"

"Yeah," he replied.

"I mean, he's a demigod, right? He must still be alive and living in Greece somewhere?"

Pav stared at me incredulously. Finally, he said, "You know they're not **real**, right?"

I stared back at him. "What?"

"They're not true stories," he continued. "They never actually **happened**, not in the way they are written."

"So Hercules never did his twelve labours and Zeus never threw thunderbolts at giants?"

Pav looked baffled. "Of course they didn't! It's all allegory."

"Ally-what?"

"It means they're stories with hidden meanings."

I stared at him but decided to leave it.

That's the difference between Pav and me: I live in the real world. And anyway, I couldn't waste time arguing with him: I had to figure out how I was going to cut a cat out of a monster's belly.

I've just gone up to bed and found my letter has vanished from under my pillow! How have I managed to lose it? It's SO annoying as now I'm going to have to write another one and I'm a busy man.

I really want Zooey to come and visit me ASAP. Not just because he'll almost certainly make me cool. But also because, well ... he's my birth dad.

SATURDAY
SEPTEMBER 9

I know what happened to the letter. I knew it as soon as I saw Mum's face at the breakfast table.

And then I **definitely** knew it when I saw the letter in her hands.

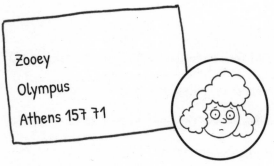

Zooey

Olympus

Athens 157 71

I was in **big** trouble. Ken was sitting on the other side of Mum, his hand placed gently on hers.

"Herc, have you secretly written to your birth father?" asked Mum.

I played it ice cool. "What makes you think it was *me*? Anyone could have written that letter."

Mum looked at me, then replied, "It was under your pillow. Plus, it's written in your handwriting."

I carried on playing it cool and shrugged.

"Plus," she added, "you wrote a return address on the back."

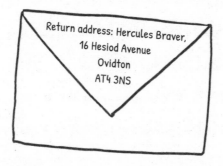

Return address: Hercules Braver,
16 Hesiod Avenue
Ovidton
AT4 3NS

"Hmmmmmm," I said, tapping my chin and buying some time. "I don't *remember...*"

Mum pursed her lips. There was a long, tense pause, the kind she normally leaves before she goes **ballistic**. I braced myself.

"Herc..." she said. "I think I owe you an apology."

Wait. "You owe *me* an apology?"

"I do," she replied. "I should have talked to you more about your birth dad."

"And how he's a rockstar?" I added.

Mum frowned. "I think you might have misinterpreted that..."

"Wait, so ... you don't mind me writing to him?"

Mum took a deep, long breath. "I just want you to be prepared. Your birth dad isn't the most ... *reliable* person. He finds it hard to think about anyone but himself..."

That's fine. I think about myself the whole time too. How else would I know how to do things like brush my teeth or practise my karate skills?

"I won't stop you from sending it. I just don't want you to get hurt."

"From what?" I asked, looking at the letter's edges. "A paper cut?"

"No," she said. "I mean if your birth dad doesn't write back."

Pfffffff. Once he reads that letter and sees how awesome I am, why **wouldn't** he write back? "So ... can I post it now?"

Mum drew in a breath then nodded. "If that's what you choose."

"Awesome!" I shouted, standing up and drumming on the table. Then I suddenly became aware of Ken sitting opposite me with a sad smile.

"Hey, buddy," he said, "why don't I walk you to the postbox?" Mum squeezed his arm and he stood up.

He walked with me to the front door and out on to the street, with about a gazillion stamps now stuck on the envelope. I could tell he wanted to say something, but he stayed silent all the way to the postbox.

I dropped the letter in and, as we turned to go home, Ken said: "I think it's great that you want to get to know your birth dad."

"OK," I replied. Then added, "Thanks."

"But I'll still always be here for you, whatever happens,"

he said, and then he hugged me.

I gave him a squeeze back. He seemed sad, and I wanted to cheer him up. I wasn't trying to get rid of him. I just wanted another, cooler version of him that would turn my luck around and impress everyone. But I thought that might be hard to explain, so I kept my mouth shut.

"I was thinking," Ken said, "why don't I take you fishing tomorrow? Spend some quality time together?"

I thought about it for a moment. "Are we fishing for sharks?"

Ken smiled like I'd made a joke. "No, just normal fish."

"Oh. Erm, sure, if you want," I said, even though it sounded a bit rubbish.

"Great," he replied. "I'll pack the fishing gear!"

And then we walked back in silence.

SUNDAY
10 SEPTEMBER

I went fishing with Ken. It was cold. But Ken seemed to enjoy it.

"My dad used to take me fishing. Isn't it magical?"

I tried to pretend that I was having a good time, while wishing I was at home planning how to catch the pond monster.

"How was your first week of big school?" asked Ken. "Have things been looking up since the little karate-chop misunderstanding?"

"Yeah. It's fine," I replied.

"I love having you there," he said, gazing at me and smiling. "I used to drop you off every day at primary school and wonder what you got up to. Now I get to see you every day!"

I gave him a smile back and said, "Thanks. I like having you there as well." Which is not entirely true. It would be a lot easier if people didn't know he was my dad. He's always drawing attention to it.

He shuffled on his seat awkwardly, then said, "You haven't been along to see my physics lab yet."

I stared into the distance. "Oh, sorry. I've just been really busy," I replied, then quickly tried to change the subject. "You know, we've been here for two hours and we still haven't caught anything."

"I've something in my bag that could help with that," he

replied.

"Is it dynamite?"

"No. It's this little guy." He pulled out something that definitely wasn't a stick of dynamite, or even a lesser explosive.

"This little baby will catch anything!" he said. "And I mean anything."

I stared at it.

And that's when a thought bomb went off in my brain.

MONDAY
11 SEPTEMBER

"I, Hercules Braver, have created the **ultimate monster-catching device!**" I declared to Hatty as we met up on the way to school.

"Is it a flaming sword?" she asked.

"It's better!" I replied and pulled it out of my bag.

"It looks like three coat hangers tied together with a stuffed cat stuck on it."

"That's **exactly** what it is!" I replied.

She looked at it long and hard. And then agreed it was the best idea I had **ever** had. "When are we going to use it?"

We turned the corner to school, and I looked at the pupils

all filing into the playground. If we could catch the pond monster now, **everyone** would see it and treat us like heroes. What's more, Pav was at a doctor's appointment so there was no one to try and talk us out of it.

Natthew cruised up. "What are you doing?"

"Catching the pond monster," I replied. "You'd better not come as it will be dangerous and you are a perfect monster-sized snack."

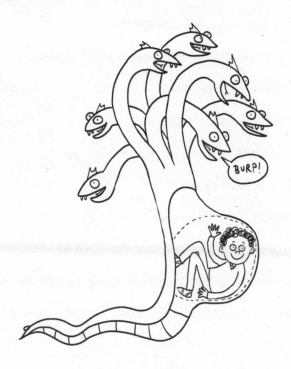

BURP!

But he followed us anyway.

"Ready?" I said to Hatty.

She nodded. Natthew gave his obligatory double thumbs up.

"Put those thumbs down," I warned. "I don't want the rope to get snagged on one."

He apologized and put them down.

I launched the hook into the pond. It landed with a *splosh* in the middle of the muddy water, then sank below. This time, I hung on tight to the other end. I wasn't going to make that mistake twice.

"Now what?" asked Hatty.

"We wait," I said confidently.

We waited.

"Waiting's boring," said Hatty.

I agreed.

"Pull it a bit, see if that gets the pond monster to take the bait."

I pulled it. Nothing happened. So I pulled it a bit more, until suddenly **the rope pulled back!**

"It's taken the bait!" I cried.

Hatty started jumping around excitedly. Kids on their way into school saw what we were doing and began to clamber through the fence to get a closer look.

"You've **got it!** You've got the **pond monster!**"

The rope was tight. I had **definitely** caught something **big**.

"Help me!" I cried. Hatty grabbed me around the waist and heaved me backwards.

By now, the noise and commotion had attracted everyone in the playground over to the pond. Natthew went on crowd control. "Stand back!" he said to everyone. "Hercules Braver has caught the **pond monster!**"

The whole school must have been there. Everyone looked dead excited.

We *heaved* backwards. Slowly - amazingly - we were dragging out the pond monster!

People were chanting!

POND MONSTER!
POND MONSTER!
POND MONSTER!

It was **awesome!** We really were going to be **heroes!** Everyone was about to know the name **Hercules Braver**, the boy who caught the legendary pond monster!

With one final heave, we yanked the rope, pulling our catch from the pond, and the force sent us tumbling backwards.

The crowd gasped. Whatever hell-creature we had dredged from the mud had shocked them into silence. I scrambled to my feet, praying that it didn't eat anyone before I could put it in a headlock.

And that's when my heart sank.

It was **worse** than a pond monster. We'd caught...

The cat cage.

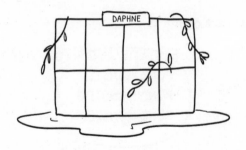

"*Ooooooo...*" said Hatty, grimacing.

"What is all this commotion? Why aren't you in lessons?" screamed a voice. It was Mr Geras, pushing through the crowd.

He marched to the front, took one look at the cat cage

and froze. He began to tremble.

I met Hatty's eyes and winced.

"Someone … *threw* Daphne's cage into the *pond...*" spluttered Mr Geras.

I dropped the rope and tried to look innocent.

His trembles of fear morphed into trembles of rage. "This is a **disgrace!** If I ever find out who stole Daphne and tried to hide the evidence..." His face was twitching, spasming almost. And I swear he was looking straight at me when he shouted: "They will be **expelled! You hear me? Expelled!**"

And with that the crowd fled. Me included.

Things took an even worse turn at break time.

I was with Pav in the playground when we were interrupted by this:

"Hello, *Herky-Werky*," said Malky, slurping on a milkshake that he wasn't allowed to have at school. "Do *you* know what happened to Mr Geras's cat?"

Nope.
Uh-uh.
Definitely not.

Malky smiled like a giant evil crocodile and brought out his phone. "Well, maybe the answer is in here."

I narrowed my eyes suspiciously. What was he talking about? Cats can't live in phones. Unless they shrink to the size of ants. And even then, it would be too dangerous with all that electricity.

He unlocked his mobile and clicked on a video. And this is where things got **really** bad.

It was shaky footage of the inside of the gym, shot from the gallery. There were four figures down below. The camera zoomed in on one, and my tummy clenched. It was **me**.

"How many times do I have to tell you? It's a **brilliant** thing I lost that cat - when we find her and hand her back to Mr Geras, he is going to think we're **awesome!**"

Malky pressed pause. "I bet Mr Geras would be **very** interested to see this."

"Where did you get this?" I squeaked.

"We were hanging out in the gym gallery on Friday when you walked in. We were filming so we could pour milkshake on you. But instead - even better - you said **this!**" A horrible grin spread over his slobbery lips. "I **told** you I was going to get you, *Herky-Werky.*"

My insides turned cold. This was a **nightmare**. If Mr Geras saw it, he'd a hundred per cent expel me. There was only one thing for it - only one thing a respectable person would do when they were about to be blackmailed.

I got down on my knees and begged, "Please don't show Mr Geras!"

"You want me to delete this video from my phone?" asked

Malky, leaning over me.

I nodded my head desperately.

"Fine. No problem. Just give me something in return."

"Fine! **Anything!** Just name it!"

"Get me *Golden Deer Quest II*," he replied.

It took a moment for it to sink in. "*Golden Deer Quest II*? Sure, but it doesn't come out for another six weeks."

"I don't **want** to wait six weeks. You have until **next Monday**."

"But ... but ... but ... it's not out then!" How am I supposed to get the most in-demand game in the **world** well over a month before it is released?

Malky shrugged. "Why don't you get your loser dad to *make* it? You're both *super-cool inventors*." Then he laughed nastily, reached up and poured his milkshake all over my head.

"*Golden Deer Quest II*. In seven days. Or I show Mr Geras." Then he turned around and walked off, leaving me in a strawberry-flavoured puddle and a whole ocean of trouble.

TUESDAY
12 SEPTEMBER

How did it all go so wrong? I had one simple wish: to win millions of new friends. Instead, everyone thinks my head smells of poo, and the school bully is blackmailing me. Now, if I don't either find Daphne or get my hands on a game that doesn't exist yet, I'm going to be **expelled**. How **unfair** is that?

We spent all afternoon looking for that cat, but she is literally **nowhere**. Hatty is still **desperate** to make some sort of trap, but we have no money to buy another cage.

And to make matters worse, my birth dad hasn't replied. Pav says it could take weeks for a letter to get to Greece. But what good is that? I need to be popular **now**.

WEDNESDAY
13 SEPTEMBER

At lunch, I was enjoying my lasagne with Hatty and Pav (and Natthew) when Malky stuck his phone in my face and played the gym video again.

"You've got five days to get me that game!" he said. "Or else!"

When he left, Pav looked strangely excited, even though we'd just been threatened by Malky. He started banging on about how this was like *another* of Other Hercules's labours. "First, he has to track down a magical lion. Then he has to fight a monster in a lake. Then he has to find and capture a deer with golden antlers, you know, a bit like *Golden Deer Quest*!"

"Wow!" said Natthew, looking amazed. But I didn't need

lessons in Greek mythology. I needed solutions.

Pav went all serious at that point and said I should just tell my parents that I'm being blackmailed, which doesn't sound like the kind of thing a Greek hero would do. If I did that, Mum would just tell Ken that I'd lost Daphne. And Ken would *surely* tell Mr Geras. And then I'd get expelled.

Hatty thinks that we should invent a time machine and go forward in time to retrieve *Golden Deer Quest II*. Which I admit is a better idea than Pav's. But when I asked how long it would take to make a time machine, she replied:

Three weeks. Two, if I don't sleep.

So that won't work either.

Either I needed to get that game, or I needed to somehow get Malky to leave me alone. I asked Pav what Greek heroes did to their enemies.

"Well," he said, thinking hard, "if you were a god, you'd just smite them."

"Smite them?"

"Yeah, smite them."

I didn't exactly know what that meant, but it sounded bad.

After school, Ken asked if I wanted to help him start his coin-sorting machine, which he's still determined to make. I didn't really, but I said that I did.

He showed me the blueprint and talked me through it. "So you load the coins on to the coin platform, which detects the weight, which activates a time delay sensor so that after ten seconds the coin tray springs closed like a lid and the sorting cylinder starts to spin really fast so that the coins fall out of the right-sized holes." He smiled proudly. "Simple, right?"

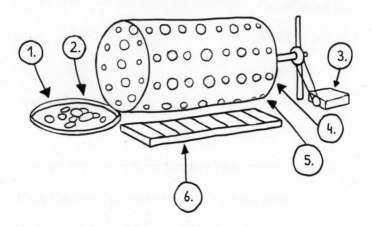

Blueprint for ridiculously complicated coin-sorting machine

1. Jumbled coins go in here
2. Spring-loaded lid detects weight and automatically closes
3. Motor starts
4. Coin-sorting drum spins
5. Coins fall out of right-sized holes
6. And into sorting boxes

"It sounds..." I searched for the right word as he smiled in anticipation. "Over-engineered..."

"You can't win the science fair with something easy!" he said, taking it as a compliment when it definitely wasn't meant as one. "I think we need to work up a prototype and try out a few techniques to..." he started to say, but I still had no idea what he was talking about or how the machine worked, so my mind wandered to Malky and my problems at school.

When he'd finished, I asked: "If I had an enemy at school, would you smite them for me?"

"Smite them?" he asked, confused.

"Yeah, smite them," I said hopefully.

He frowned. "Is everything OK at school, Herc? You know you can tell me if it isn't."

I hesitated for a second, but I knew it would just get me in even more trouble if I told him. Ken would never smite anyone for me. Let's face it: he's not the kind of dad you'd want in your corner if you needed to win a fight.

THURSDAY
14 SEPTEMBER

I don't think Mr Geras has slept since Daphne went missing.
He looks dangerously on the edge.

He's even started talking about getting the police involved
and pressing criminal charges when he finds the culprit.

Can you go to jail for throwing a cat cage into a pond?
Pav says no but Hatty says definitely yes, so I don't know who
to believe.

Malky is still goading me. There's no way I can get him
Golden Deer Quest II by Monday. Especially as Hatty's time
machine is just a box with some phone chargers stuck into it.

So I'm **doomed.**

On top of everything else, Ken did a school assembly all about the science fair and started talking about how it was my idea to invent a coin-sorting machine, and how much I love science and inventing stuff. **Everyone** was sniggering. He's just **so bad** for my image. I **wish, wish, wish** my rockstar dad would turn up and show everyone how cool I really am. I bet he'd get Malky to leave me alone.

After school, I just lay on my bed, staring at the ceiling. I hadn't felt so bad since I was stuck inside that vending machine.

Mum popped her head around the door. "Just going out to the shops. Want anything?"

Where to start: Daphne? *Golden Deer Quest II?* Something to smite Malky with? A letter from my birth dad?

Instead I just said wearily, "No thanks."

Mum pulled her concerned face. "Herc? Is this about your letter to your dad?"

"Partly."

She sighed, perched next to me, and stroked my hair. "Your birth dad isn't the most thoughtful person." And then she got all mushy. "It's only right to wonder about him. But remember, whether he writes back or not: I love you and Ken loves you."

"Do you think he'll *ever* write back?"

She smiled a sad smile. "I couldn't stop you writing to him, Herc. But this was my biggest worry: that it would leave you feeling like this." She thought for a second, then laughed and said, "Actually, my biggest worry was that he would **turn** up!" She seemed to disappear into herself for a moment, as if imagining what that would be like, before snapping to with a shudder. "How about I get you some ice cream to cheer you up?"

She headed downstairs and I heard the front door go. I was lying there, wondering why she wouldn't want him to turn up, when the doorbell went. No doubt Mum had forgotten her keys.

I heaved myself out of bed and headed downstairs. I opened the door and—

It wasn't Mum.

Instead, a tall man with deeply tanned skin, flowing grey-and-white hair and a sculpted salt-and-pepper beard stood there. He was wearing a white linen shirt and trousers and black aviator glasses and looked like some sort of film star.

"Erm, hello?" I said.

He flashed me a smile with teeth so white they almost blinded me. Then he lowered his glasses, and I swear I could see a twinkle in his bright-blue eyes. And that's when he pulled something out of his pocket. My mouth fell open. It was my letter.

"Hello, Hercules," he said, his voice deep and syrupy like treacle. "I am Zooey, **your father.**"

What the?! I opened my mouth, but no noise came out.

Instead, there was the sound of a handbag hitting the pavement. And that was when I saw Mum, white as a sheet, staring at us.

"You came," she said. "I **never** thought you'd come."

But he **has**. It has *actually* happened! For once, something has gone right for me!

My birth dad has come to visit me, and he is even more awesome than I imagined!

We sat at the kitchen table while Mum made two cups of tea with a face like she'd seen a very tall ghost. I stared at the bronzed man-mountain opposite me.

I **can't believe** he's come! He is **everything** I imagined he might be. He looks like a **movie star** or a **wrestler** or at the very least a breakfast TV presenter. There were so many things I wanted to say to him, but the most important was:

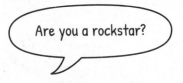

Are you a rockstar?

"Kind of..." he said with a thick accent that must be Greek. Then he laughed a deep laugh that made his shoulders heave. "Some say I am a **god**."

Mum spat out her tea. "*Zooey!*"

A **god**! What a **cool** way to describe yourself. *A god of what?* I wonder. A god of rock?

"It is very good to meet you at last, Hercules," he said. "Do you know that I gave you that name?"

I nodded, unable to pull my eyes from him.

"It has always been my **favourite** name. I am thinking, now I'm over from Greece, that you and I should spend some time together."

I nodded even faster.

Quality time

Mum folded her arms. She was about to say something, but the sound of the front door stopped her.

Ken walked in, and Zooey raised an eyebrow. "This must be the Ken you mention?" He looked at Mum with a tiny smile in the corners of his lips and she looked away and said between gritted teeth, "Ken, meet Zooey."

Ken looked momentarily shocked. "Hello... Welcome! Herky-Werky here has been very excited to meet you."

"*Herky-Werky?*" said Zooey. Then he looked at me and I quickly rolled my eyes, but made sure Ken didn't see.

Ken pulled up a chair next to Zooey. I looked at Zooey and Ken side by side.

Ken is a nice dad, don't get me wrong, but if I could choose which of their DNA I want pumping through my veins, then I'm obviously going to go with the guy who looks like he's been **carved from oak**. Not the guy who looks like he burrows underground.

"So, Zooey, did you fly over?" asked Ken, trying to make chitchat.

Zooey smiled. The lines on his leathery face wrinkled. "Yes. On a chariot."

Ken frowned. "Is that a model of private jet?"

"In a manner of speaking," replied Zooey.

Wow! A private jet!

"Anyone for olives?" asked Zooey. Then, seemingly from nowhere, he whipped out a bowl of olives.

I **love** olives. I grabbed a handful and stuffed them in my mouth.

Ken looked around, puzzled. "Where did you get those from?"

Zooey smiled, then threw an olive high in the air, tilted his head back and caught it between his teeth. "Hmmmmm. **Kalamata!**" he said, swallowing it and smacking his lips.

It was **so cool.** I grabbed a handful and did the same.

I don't know what "Kalamata!" means, but it's a great catchphrase!

Zooey fixed his eyes on Mum as she sat down next to me.

"You are looking **very** well, Sarah."

Her cheeks went red. I couldn't tell if she was blushing or angry. I think angry.

Ken adjusted his glasses and asked Zooey what he did in Greece.

"I own some bars and nightclubs," he replied, not taking his eyes from Mum.

I grabbed another handful of olives. It was amazing: *however* many I took, the bowl **always** seemed full.

Then Ken asked Zooey how long he planned to stay.

Zooey shrugged. He was still looking at Mum, who was staring down at the table. Finally, he replied, "I am thinking a few weeks. A month. Two, maybe. To get to know Hercules properly."

I drummed my hands on the table. **"Kalamata!"**

Ken fiddled with his glasses again. It's something he does when he's anxious. "That'd be really nice. I think it's important you two get to know each other." He glanced at Mum, who looked incredibly on edge. "Don't you think, darling?"

There was a long silence. We all stared at Mum.

Finally she said, "Fine. But..." She lowered her voice. "Zooey. Do **not** hurt him."

Zooey flashed her a wink and smiled. "Of course not."

And I smiled as well. Mum must have forgotten about my purple belt in karate! It'll more likely be **me** hurting *him*!

FRIDAY
15 SEPTEMBER

Today has been one of the **best** days of my life!

Mum agreed to let Zooey pick me up from school for the next few weeks so we can hang out in the afternoon. How **awesome** is that?

After the last lesson, I waited with Pav and Hatty, describing Zooey to them. I'd been banging on all day about how awesome he is. "He's **so** tall. Probably ... as tall as that lamp post. And **strong**. He can bench lift two tonnes!" (It's possible that I've been getting a *tiny* bit carried away with how impressive he is.) "And he runs hundreds of nightclubs and says that he is kind of a rockstar."

Pav stared at me. "He sounds ... *unbelievable.*"

"I **know**, right!"

He scowled. "Not *amazing*-unbelievable. *Unbelievable*-unbelievable. No one can bench lift two tonnes. And no one is as tall as a lamp post."

"And how can you be *kind of* a rockstar?" asked Hatty. "Does he have rockstar legs but not rockstar arms? Or a rockstar bottom but not rockstar ears?"

I was about to explain that maybe he is retired or maybe he is a DJ or something, when a figured loomed behind us. I knew immediately it was Malky.

"Got my game yet, *Herky-Werky*?"

"Not yet," I replied.

"Well, you've got until Monday to get it to me, *loser!*" he said with stinky breath.

I'd had enough of him. "I am **not** a loser!" I shouted. "I am a total **legend** and my dad is a total **legend** and my friends are total **legends**." Well, maybe not Natthew, but no need to go into details.

Malky laughed. "Your dad is the biggest **loser** of them

all. He's bald and has got glasses thicker than a fridge and..."
He was going to carry on when the roar of an engine cut him off.

We all turned to look. A gold-plated sports car pulled up outside the gates. The door opened with a hiss and clouds of dry ice spilled out, followed by a sandalled foot, a white-linen trouser leg, and finally ... Zooey. I felt a surge of excitement like electricity.

"Sorry, guys, gotta go - my **dad's** here!"

"**That's** your dad?" gawped Malky. "But your dad is Mr Braver the physics teacher..."

"He's my *step*dad. This is my birth dad." I slung my jacket over my shoulders and strolled out of the school. Everyone stared at me – even Billy and Ben, the cool kids, their mouths hanging open. I high-fived Zooey and clambered on to the passenger seat. With a roar of the engine, we zoomed off, leaving Ken behind, who had pulled up on his tandem bike to let us past. He gave a little wave, but we were going too fast for me to wave back.

Zooey's gold sports car is **amazing**. It has crocodile-skin seats and a diamond gear stick.

"How did you get so rich?" I asked.

He laughed. "I created money."

Wow, I thought. Maybe he started a cryptocurrency or something.

"Hey, check the glovebox."

I popped it open and found another huge bowl of olives.

"**Kalamata!**" I cried.

"Who was that friend you were speaking with?"

"Oh, that's Pav."

He smiled. "I have big, strong friends too. Mount Olympus is filled with them." Mount Olympus must be one of his nightclubs. Though there are many ways I'd describe Pav, and big and strong aren't among them. But then I realized who he was talking about.

"Oh, *Malky!* He's not my friend. He's a big, horrible giant who's hassling me."

The laughter drained from Zooey's face. "Giants? I **hate** giants!"

"Me too!" I said, stuffing olives in my mouth.

He seemed to think for a while. "What does he want from you, this giant?"

Weeeeeell. I took a deep breath and told him all about Malky, the video, Daphne and Golden Deer Hunt II. "It's an impossible task. He's set me up to fail. It's completely **ruining** my life."

124

Zooey muttered something under his breath. It sounded like, "*I do not usually negotiate with giants.*" Then he said more clearly, "Open the glovebox again. I have a surprise for you. At the back."

I reached my hand in and my fingers wrapped around something hard and rectangular. I pulled it out.

"What?! But *how*?"

"That will stop the giant," he said.

How incredible is *that*?

"You are the coolest dad in the universe!"

Then he looked at me over his aviators and said, "Wanna go bowling?"

At bowling, Zooey got a strike with every ball. One time, the two back side pins were still left standing. But then, a second later - as if they were scared of disappointing him - they fell over.

"How did you do that?" I asked, my mouth hanging open.

Magic!

Everyone in the bowling alley stared at us in awe - including a group of kids from my school.

"Who *is* that?" asked one.

"My dad!" I replied.

"He is **amazing!**"

"Yeah," I said. He's even more amazing than I ever imagined!

At the end of the game, the manager came out to shake hands with Zooey. They asked him if he's a pro. He said he's not. I told that manager that I am a pro - or, at least, that I am thinking about becoming a pro. He looked like he didn't believe either of us.

As he left, I said to Zooey: "You are an absolute god at bowling!"

"Not just bowling," he replied, in a low voice. "I am a god of **everything**!"

"Even paintballing?"

"Even paintballing."

Then he raised his voice and shouted: "Milkshakes on me!" And everyone cheered.

Kalamata!

On the way home, I chucked quick-fire questions at Zooey.

"How come you are **SO** cool?"

"I invented cool."

"Were you **always** this cool?"

"Ever since I took over The Heavens." (I think that must be another one of his nightclubs.)

"Can I be as cool as you?"

"Of course. You are my son."

"Can we stop for a burger?"

"Just look in the glovebox."

I opened the glovebox. Zooey really had thought of **everything**.

The glovebox must have a heating element or something because it was piping hot. I bit down and it was the **best burger** I've ever tasted.

"Who made *this*?"

"Hestia," he replied, which must be a secret new fast-food place, because I've never heard of it.

Then Zooey started asking *me* loads of questions. It shows what a thoughtful guy he is that he is so interested in my life. Most of the questions were about Mum, but obviously she's a big part of my life.

"Does your mother ever mention me?"

"Sometimes," I said, with a mouth full of burger.

"What does she say?"

"That you live in Greece and you are kind of famous."

"Did she say why?"

"Not really. She mentioned that you might have been a rockstar? In a manner of speaking."

"Interesting," he muttered. "And tell me about this Ken."

"Oh. Ken's a really nice guy. He's just a bit..."

Zooey finished my sentence: "... of a *loser.*"

A bit harsh but not a *million* miles off. "He's not very cool, no. Not like you."

"Is your mother happy?"

"Not when I do things like nearly break my wrist by accidentally karate-chopping Malky's shoulder. Or get stuck inside a vending machine."

"No, I mean with Ken."

"Oh - yeah, I think so."

And then he muttered something, but I couldn't hear him because I was chewing down on my burger.

*

When Zooey pulled up outside our house, I could see Mum peeking through the front room curtains.

"Catch you on Monday!" I said. Then I climbed out, and he roared off down the street.

Mum was waiting to ambush me, fiddling nervously with her wedding ring. "How ... was it?"

"Zooey is ... **awesome**!" I replied. I told her all about the bowling and the milkshake and the burgers.

Mum stayed silent. Then she glanced up the stairs towards Ken's workshop and lowered her voice. "Did he tell you anything ... *secret*?"

I stared at her. What was she getting at?

"I don't think so..." I said. "There's this *amazing* burger place called Hestia that I've *never* heard of."

She looked at me long and hard, like that wasn't the answer she was after. Finally, she said, "OK." Then she paused before getting all mushy. "I know you probably think I'm worrying for no reason, Herc, but all I want is to keep you safe and happy. You're my world." Then she gave me a long hug.

I don't know what she's worried about. Having Zooey here is the best thing that's **ever happened to me**.

She let go and whispered, "Make sure you say hi to Ken. I think he's feeling a bit... Just say hi, OK?"

I went up and stuck my head in Ken's workshop.

"Hey, Herky!" he said, while staring thoughtfully at the prototype of his coin-sorting machine. "This isn't working exactly as I want it to."

Of course it isn't, I thought. He'd made it more complicated than the moon landings.

"The spring-loaded lid isn't tuned right. Either it doesn't close at all, or it snaps shut and fires the coins everywhere and I can't get it open again..."

He stared at it some more, tapping his chin in thought. Then he suddenly seemed to remember where I'd been. "How was your afternoon with Zooey?"

"It was the best day **ever**!" I blurted out.

"Ah, that's great!" Ken forced a smile. Then he stared back at his coin machine, deep in thought ... about how to fix it, I hoped, not about what a great time I'd had with Zooey.

I stood there feeling really guilty because I never sounded that excited about his fishing trips. But how can a fishing trip compare to having Zooey around?

MONDAY
18 SEPTEMBER

I strutted into the playground this morning, with *Golden Deer Quest II* in my bag.

Pav and Hatty met me by the gates.

"Today's the day!" Pav whimpered. "What are you going to do?"

"I'm going to give Malky **this**," I replied, unveiling the game.

"But ... **how**...?" spluttered Pav.

"You invented a time machine, didn't you?" shouted Hatty. "You went to the future!" Then she looked around, eyes wide. "Wait. Is *this* the future?"

"Nope," I said. "**Zooey** gave it to me."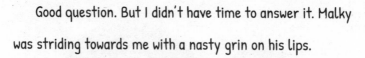

They both fell silent.

"H-h-how did he get it so early?" spluttered Pav.

Good question. But I didn't have time to answer it. Malky was striding towards me with a nasty grin on his lips.

"Got my game, *Herky-Werky*?"

I *whipped* out *Golden Deer Quest II*.

But Malky didn't look happy. In fact, he looked the *opposite* of happy.

"That's impossible..." he muttered.

"Nothing's impossible!" I replied. "Not for **Hercules Braver**!"

"Actually, you can't eat your own mouth," interjected Hatty.

Malky continued to stare at the game, nostrils flaring.

"Now you delete the video," I said. "That was the deal."

He didn't move.

"I wanted to get you, Braver. I wanted to get you so badly," he seethed.

But then something occurred to him that made him smile. *Not* a nice smile. "Fine. I *will* delete that video from my phone."

"Thank you!" I said.

He held his phone up, opened the video and pressed delete.

I punched the air.

"However," continued Malky, the nasty grin growing, "I didn't say **anything** about the copy of the video on my computer."

What? "Hang on, that's not fair! You can't go back on your word."

"Just try and stop me," he replied. "I don't like you, Braver. I told you I'm going to get you, so that's what I'm going to do."

I fell to my knees. "Noooooooooooooo!"

Now I'm waiting to be picked up from school. Today can't end soon enough. Just **how** can things have gone from so good to so bad so quickly? Malky is determined to destroy me, and Mr Geras is raging because Daphne is still AWOL.

I'm doomed.

Zooey picked me up from school. But this time, when he pulled up in his gold sports car, I struggled to get excited. How could I, when Malky would be showing the video to Mr Geras first thing tomorrow?

Zooey looked at me over his sunglasses. "Want to go to the BMX track?"

"OK," I said, with a shrug.

"Great! Hey, you will tell your mum how much **fun** we are

having together and what a **great guy** I am, won't you?"

I shrugged. "Sure."

He grinned. Then he put his foot down on the accelerator and we screeched off.

At the BMX track, Zooey got a park record for doing a **three-thousand-six-hundred-degree** backflip. That's when you do **ten** somersaults without touching the ground.

The park manager said he **didn't even know that move was possible** without suspending gravity. Zooey winked at me and whispered: "That's exactly what I did."

I was still feeling a bit depressed about the whole Malky situation, so I didn't do any backflips. Even though I could have if I'd wanted.

Afterwards we sat down on a bench on a hill overlooking the town. I still felt rubbish. I thought that Zooey turning up would solve my problems. Sure, everyone thinks I have an awesome rockstar dad - but what does that matter if I get expelled?

"What bothers you?" asked Zooey.

I took a deep breath and said, "What do **you** do when somebody goes back on their word?"

A dark cloud crossed his face. "I strap them to a rock so that a vulture can feast on their liver **for all eternity.**" Which seems a bit harsh, but maybe it's a Greek proverb or something.

"It's just, the giant I was telling you about has decided

he's going to dob me in to the headmaster *even though* I gave him the game."

Another dark cloud passed over Zooey's face. And this time, I mean **literally**. All these grey storm clouds were gathering directly over the town. Like, really, really quickly. Quicker than I've ever seen.

"Then the headmaster will expel me," I continued.

Zooey muttered to himself, his face contorted with rage. "I **hate** people who go back on their word. And I **hate** giants."

The storm clouds blocked out the sun.

"Shall we go?" I said. "I think it might rain." But Zooey wasn't listening.

"I will solve this for you, my son," he said.

"How?" I frowned.

And that's when things got **really** weird.

He stood up, thrust his hands into the air and started shouting at the clouds.

"I, Zeus, King of the Gods, Cloud Gatherer and Lord of Storms, do smite you..."

He looked down at me. "What did you say his name was?"

"Erm..." Maybe this was one of his rockstar acts that he does onstage? "He's called Malky. Not sure of his surname."

"I, Zeus, King of the Gods, Cloud Gatherer and Lord of Storms, do smite you ... Malky ... bringing thunder, lightning and destruction upon your abode."

Erm ... what are you doing?

I was about to ask a pretty obvious question.

But then the **weirdest, scariest,** most **incredible** thing in my whole life happened. A roar of thunder **ripped** through the sky, and as Zooey stood

there - hands held wide, the wind billowing through his hair -
a **huge bolt of lightning** crashed down from the
clouds and struck a house.

What the...?!

I leapt out of my seat. "Y-y-y-y-y-you just did that?
How...? How did you...? How did you do that?" *It* **must** *be a*
coincidence, I thought. But **what** a coincidence!

Half the house had collapsed. Only one wall remained.
Then Zooey swiped a hand through the air, and a **second**

bolt exploded the last bit of brickwork.

I was stunned. Speechless.

Zooey sat down, a satisfied smile on his face. The grey clouds parted as quickly as they had appeared. Sunlight flooded the park. Birds chirped. In the distance, sirens howled.

I looked down at the town and the smouldering remains.

Finally, I managed to spit out the words, "Who ... whose house did you just destroy?"

"That giant you spoke of. Milky ... Malky."

"Is he **dead**?!"

Zooey frowned. "Did you not **want** him dead?"

"No! I hate him, but I didn't want to *kill* him. I just wanted you to smite him!"

"Then consider him smote."

"But he's alive, right?" I asked desperately.

"Indeed. The home was empty," replied Zooey, surveying the town, his chest puffed out.

I gazed at his smouldering house in slight relief. But

still! I mean, Malky is a giant pain in the butt, but I'm not sure he deserved **that**. Then I thought of Zooey standing up and summoning that storm and my whole body jangled with excitement.

I turned back to him. "Who *are* you?"

He frowned, like it was obvious. "Why, I am **Zeus, King of the Gods**, of course."

And that's when I think I must have fainted.

When I came to, I was sitting on the park bench, my head spinning.

"You're Zeus?"

"Yes."

"The real Zeus, from those Greek myths?"

"Yes."

"But Pav says you're not real."

"I am very real, I assure you."

I was babbling. I couldn't process it all. "But ... but ... but ...

Pav says you're an allergy."

He raised one eyebrow. "You mean an allegory?"

"Yeah, that."

He laughed a deep laugh. "Foolish humans."

I still couldn't get my head around what was happening.

"Do you not believe me?"

"I... I... I..."

He clicked his fingers, there was a little flash, and suddenly it wasn't Zooey sitting in front of me but a giant eagle. This was so **trippy**.

"Believe me now?" said the eagle. And then with a flash he shapeshifted back into a human. "Could a normal man throw lightning or change form?"

I shook my head slowly. "No." There was no other explanation. "You ... you ... you **must** be Zeus." It felt weird even saying it.

He looked pleased and nodded. "I am."

I stared at him in stunned silence, my head spinning. Finally, I said, "Why didn't you tell me earlier?"

Zooey looked at me like I was being dim. "I dropped some pretty big hints."

"Such as?"

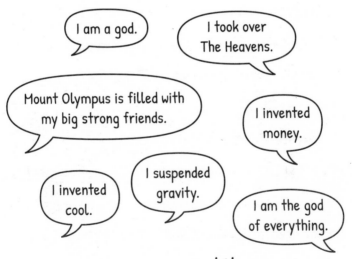

I am a god.

I took over The Heavens.

Mount Olympus is filled with my big strong friends.

I invented money.

I invented cool.

I suspended gravity.

I am the god of everything.

I still think he could have been a **bit** clearer.

"So, if you are Zeus..." I could feel the jigsaw pieces connecting in my head. "I am ... the son of a **god**?"

He nodded.

I rolled the words around my tongue: *"I am the son of a god."* Then a surge of excitement shot through my body, making every bit of me tingle. **I am the son of a god!**

"So you are my dad **and** Other Hercules's dad? Does that mean..." My head spun more. "Am I going to grow up like him?"

Zeus tilted his head back and laughed so hard his shoulders heaved. "I wouldn't have thought so!" he said, wiping an eye and looking at my muscles. "I have many, many children. I just thought it was time to use that name again. Hercules was one of my most favourite sons."

"Like me?"

He looked to the horizon and didn't answer.

My mind whirred with possibilities. "Does this mean I have **magical powers** or **super strength**?" I looked at my fingers, expecting sparks to come out of them.

Zeus shrugged. "Not always. Some of my many children have been **gods** and **goddesses**. Others heroes and heroines. But some have been everyday people."

I started thinking about **everything** I could do with Zeus as my dad. Like ... maybe I can arrive at school on a winged chariot.

Or scare Malky into leaving me alone.

GRRRRR!

"I can't wait to tell everyone that Zeus is **back**. And I'm his son! **Kalamata!**"

He frowned and held his palms up. "Do not be so hasty. People in this world stopped believing in me a long time ago. And I am better for it. Humankind is..." He groped for the right word. "... *hassle*."

"Hassle?"

"Hassle." Zooey put a hand on my shoulder. At first, I thought maybe he was going to bestow some killer new powers on me, but he just said, "Son, what say we keep this a secret? *Our* secret."

"I can't tell anyone?" I replied, deflating. What's the point of having a god as a dad if you can't lord it over people?

"Our secret," he said, squeezing my shoulder tighter.

I was a bit annoyed at first. If everyone knew I was a demigod, then I'd one hundred per cent be the most popular kid in school. But then I thought about how awesome it was that me and Zooey had this major *secret* between us.

"We can still be awesome together, though, can't we?" I said, tingling with excitement.

"Of course we can," said Zooey. "And then you can tell your mum how much fun you are having with me."

Deal! Kalamata!

TUESDAY
19 SEPTEMBER

I woke up this morning, leapt out of bed and karate-chopped the air.

I have a god as a father!

Last night, I frantically googled everything I possibly could about Zeus. I wish I'd been listening more when Pav went on and on about him. I learnt that:

He rules the universe from Mount Olympus, which **isn't** a nightclub and **is** an awesome mountain in Greece where he and the other eleven Greek gods, called the Olympians, hang out - and they are all part of his (*our!*) family.

And he instructed his brother Prometheus to make all of humankind! How awesome is that? That's sooooo much more impressive than a coin-sorting machine. I also started

reading about some of the people Zooey had got angry with and punished. Turns out that Malky got off lightly! Zooey strapped one guy to a burning wheel for all of eternity, which must have **really** sucked. I was on a hot Ferris wheel for a whole ten minutes once and that was *pretty* bad.

When I finally fell asleep, I dreamt of Zooey and me on Mount Olympus hanging out with all the other Olympians, drinking unlimited Pepsi and not having to go to bed because we are all **gods** and can do whatever we want (or half god, in my case).

I headed downstairs this morning whistling a jaunty tune. Mum was out last night when I got home, and I could tell she wanted to grill me about Zooey ... again.

"How was Zooey?" she asked.

"As **awesome** as ever," I replied.

She shifted nervously. "You'd let me know if he ... *told* you anything out of the ordinary, wouldn't you?"

"Erm, sure." I felt a bit bad for lying, but I *had* promised Zooey that I'd keep his identity a secret.

Mum's eyes were strained. "OK. Just be careful. I don't want spending time with Zooey to…" She seemed to consider her words. "… confuse you."

Confuse me? I've never been less confused in my life! I've always known I'm **awesome**. And now Zooey has turned up to prove me one hundred per cent correct!

In the playground, all **everyone** could talk about was Malky's house getting destroyed by lightning last night. He wasn't at school - apparently he is staying with relatives out of town. Not only was his house destroyed, but lots of his belongings too, including his mobile and computer - erasing all evidence of me confessing to losing Daphne. I am **off the hook**!

"It's practically a **miracle**," said Hatty.

"Yeah," agreed Pav. "Like **divine intervention** or something."

I bit my lip and tried not to say anything.

"I mean, just as he is about to dob you in!" continued Hatty. **"What are the chances?"**

Staying silent was **killing** me. But I **promised** I wouldn't tell a soul about Zooey's true identity.

"It's like something out of a **Greek myth**, isn't it, Pav?" said Hatty. "Who is that god who controls lightning?"

"Zeus!" replied Pav, who never gets excited about anything but was pumped about this. "Like, this one time, there was an evil king called Salmoneus who was impersonating Zeus, so he killed him with a lightning bolt! It's like that!"

"That is so cool!" said Hatty.

It was **SO** hard not telling them. Because, more than anything, I wanted Pav's advice on what cool stuff I should do with Zooey. I played it breezy and said, "If Zeus *was* real – which he's one hundred per cent **not** – what would you get him to do?"

"Oooooh, good question," said Pav, tapping his chin. Then his eyes sprang wide open. "I know! I'd get him to grant me some wishes."

Now it was time for *my* eyes to spring wide open. "**Really?** Zeus can grant *wishes*?"

Pav nodded. "He sure can!" Then he gave a little chuckle. "But you have to be careful what you wish for!"

"How come?"

"Well..." he said. Then he started to tell us one of his Greek myths.

This one time, Zeus was spying on this girl he liked called Semele.

When Eros shot him with one of his love arrows.

"Wait," said Hatty. "Who is Eros?"

"You probably know him by his Roman name - Cupid," replied Pav. "If he shoots an arrow at you and you are looking at someone, you fall instantly in love with them."

"Oh," said Hatty. "So you have no choice? Isn't that a bit creepy?"

"Yeah, well," said Pav, annoyed at the interruption. "Greek gods could be *creepy* and selfish and all other kinds of bad things."

"Fine. Continue," said Hatty.

Zeus fell instantly in love with Semele.

They started dating but when Zeus's wife Hera found out, she was furious.

So Hera disguised herself as an old woman and told Semele of Zeus's true identity. But Semele didn't believe she was going out with the King of the Gods.

I swear on the River Styx to grant you your wish.

So, the next time she saw Zeus she asked that he grant her a wish and he swore he would.

She asked that he reveal his true self. The trouble is, no mortal could see a god as powerful as Zeus in his true form and survive.

But he had sworn an oath. So he had to grant the wish. He turned into his godlike form and Semele got burnt to a crisp by one of his lightning bolts.

"That's the end of the story?" I said. "She got burnt to a crisp?"

"Hang on," said Hatty. "If he really liked her, and he knew it was going to kill her, why didn't he refuse to transform?"

Pav shrugged. "Because although the Greek gods could be sneaky and selfish at times, if they swore an oath on the River Styx, they had to fulfil it or they would be chucked off Mount Olympus."

How **honourable**. That's **so** like Zooey. And also, **so** like me. Well, most of the time.

"So, if Zeus **was** still around – which he completely isn't – you'd ask him for infinite wishes?"

Pav narrowed his eyes suspiciously. "I'm not sure he'd grant *infinite* wishes but ... yes, in theory."

My head was about to burst.

Because now I know how I'm going to solve **all** my problems.

WEDNESDAY
20 SEPTEMBER

Mega annoyingly, I couldn't see Zooey last night to ask him for infinite wishes because I promised Mum I'd miss a day to help Ken with his super-complicated coin-sorting machine. It *still* isn't working properly.

So today is the day I'm going to ask him! Will tell you how it goes.

Zooey picked me up from school in his gold car. I climbed into the passenger seat feeling suddenly nervous.

Zooey high-fived me, then said, "Tell me, how is your mother? Does she talk of me?"

"Um. *Sort of,*" I replied. "But not much."

"*Really?!* I find that most strange." He went to start the car.

158

I took a deep breath and said: "You know how you are a **god**?"

"**King** of the gods," he replied.

"Yeah, king of the gods..." My heart was in my mouth. "Can you, um, *grant wishes*?"

He let go of the keys. "I don't do that any more."

"You did it for Semolina."

"You mean Semele? That's why I stopped. Terrible ending. The smell stayed in my nostrils for months."

I sensed he was reluctant. Which is fair enough if you accidentally burnt someone you liked to a crisp. So I needed to tread carefully, subtly persuade him to change his mind.

I paused, took a breath and said: "**Please** can I have some wishes? Please. Please. **Pretty please!**"

Zooey stared at me in thought. Was he cracking?

I clasped my hands together in a begging gesture. "I'll do anything. **Please!**"

Then a smile curled in the corner of his lips. "I'll tell you what, my son. I will make you a deal."

"**Anything!**" What was he going to ask me to do? Smite some monsters for him? Retrieve a golden fleece?

"Get your mother to come for a coffee with me."

Wait. *What?* "Come again?"

"Get your mother to come for a coffee with me."

"*That's it?*"

"That's it."

"And I can have infinite wishes?"

"Not infinite."

"Ten!"

"Two."

"Six!"

"Four. And no wishing for more wishes."

"Deal!" I said. "Will you swear it?"

I swear on the River Styx to grant you, Hercules Braver, four wishes.

I couldn't believe it! I had four wishes! **Four!** And all I had to do was get my mum to go for a coffee with him?! He **completely** lowballed me there!

"So, any idea what you would like to wish for?"

I smiled. Malky's video was gone. Now it was time to wave the rest of my problems goodbye.

I took Zooey over to the pond.

"You *really* want to use your first wish on *this*? Clearing out a pond?"

"Yup!" I replied. If I fixed up this filthy pond, Mr Geras would think I was a **hero**. Plus, I could capture that monster once and for all and become a school legend!

"Fine," he said. "Then we're going to need assistance."

"From who?"

"**'ello!**" A scruffy bloke with a beard who smelt of seaweed appeared behind us. He was smiling and holding a pitchfork.

"Water is not my domain," said Zooey. "So, Hercules: meet your uncle, Poseidon."

What?!

"As in Poseidon, god of the seas?" I felt like my head might explode.

The scruffy man tapped his name badge. "Call me Donny."

O.M.G. If the last few days weren't wild enough ... now I was meeting some of the other Greek gods?

"Brother, could you help us clean this pond? It is one of Hercules's wishes."

Donny raised an eyebrow. "*Hercules?*"

"Not that one."

"And his wish is: *to clean out a pond?*"

Sure is!

Donny leant on his pitchfork, sucked his moustache, and inspected the pond. "You're looking at a sludge tanker, new liner, deep clean."

"And there's a **monster** in there," I said.

"Oooof. I've got a monster surcharge. Whole lot is gonna cost three thousand pounds."

He looked from Zooey to me to Zooey to me, then elbowed me playfully in the ribs. "Just pulling your leg."

Then he thrust his pitchfork into the air, and instantly a whirlpool swished around the pond, the water levels dropping like someone had pulled the plug out. With a gurgle, the last bit of muddy water drained out of a little hole at the bottom, leaving just a big brown crater with a giant, revolting frog at the bottom.

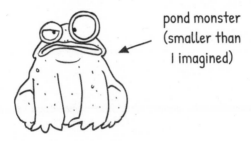

pond monster (smaller than I imagined)

"There's your monster!" Donny laughed.

It jumped out beside our feet. Daphne was **definitely** not inside its belly. I stared at it and winced. Whichever way I tried to spin it, capturing a frog was not going to achieve me legend status at school.

Donny pointed at it. "You wanna smite it?"

"Smite it?" I asked.

"Go on, smite it!" said Zooey. "Smite it good, son."

"Chop its head off!" said Donny.

"Rip it to pieces!" chimed Zooey.

"We love a good smiting in this family!" Donny chuckled.

I hesitated. I'm all up for killing dragons and gorgons, but not podgy pond frogs. "I'm not sure I want to."

"Is he definitely one of *yours*, brother?" Donny asked with grin. Then he rolled his shoulders and said, "Right, let's get this pond looking good."

He thrust his pitchfork in the air once more, and suddenly beautiful, crystal-clear water bubbled forth from the hole at the bottom, and bullrushes and waterlilies sprang up.

"This do ya?" asked Donny.

Would it? Wishes are the **best**.

"Thanks, Zooey!" I said, giving his arm a little hug, which seemed to surprise him as he went a bit tense. "And thanks, Donny," I said, as he slung me a salute, then disappeared in a puff of smoke.

"Any other wishes?" asked Zooey.

"I need to find a missing cat," I said.

Zooey looked at me like I was pulling his leg. "What?"

"That one," I said, pointing at one of Daphne's "Missing" posters.

"Fine. Do you wish it? You must say that you wish it."

"I **wish** for you to bring back Daphne."

Zooey clicked his fingers and suddenly, in a flash of light, Daphne appeared at my feet. I picked her up and she purred.

Just like that, **all** my problems were solved. Malky and his video had gone. The monster may not exist, but the pond was cleared. Daphne was back. And I still had two wishes left. Having a god as a dad is the **best**! How did I **ever** manage before with just Ken?

"Any more wishes?" asked Zooey.

I thought about all the things I could wish for: infinite money ... world peace ... Pav to be less grumpy. Then I looked across the playground where Billy and Ben were walking to the music room for band practice, guitar cases strapped to their backs, effortlessly passing a football to one another and laughing.

I didn't need to think twice about it. I knew exactly

what my third wish was going to be. "Zooey, make me the **coolest** kid in the school."

Zooey took me to a salon I'd never seen before, down a back street in town.

"What are we doing here?" I asked, popping Daphne down on the floor, inside a cardboard box I'd fashioned into a cat cage.

"Waiting for someone," he replied.

"Who?"

"You'll see." He picked up a comb and ran it through his long, shiny hair as he stared into a mirror. He asked the same question he always does: "So you're sure your mother hasn't been saying how **amazing** and **all-powerful** I am?"

"Um. No. Not really."

He looked momentarily put out. Then he carried on combing his hair. "You know, she is as beautiful as she was when I first met her."

...m? Beautiful? I suppose she is. I've never really thought about it.

"It is unfathomable to me that she would marry someone like Ken."

I didn't want to argue, but he was being a bit harsh. "He's not the coolest. He is a nice guy, though."

"*How* is he a nice guy?" asked Zooey, moving on to combing his beard.

"Well..." I thought for a bit. "I guess he's always saying nice things about how great I am."

Zooey guffawed and looked at me. "Really?" He wrapped his thumb and forefinger around my bicep. "You are so small. So weak!"

"Well, Mum wouldn't buy me a weights set..." I started to say, but Zooey talked over me.

"No, no, no. This is **not** what greatness looks like at all..." The bell above the door rang and Zooey glanced up. "On which note!"

168

"Hiya, Dad!" said a woman with huge hair, massive eyelashes and long pink fingernails.

"Aphrodite, meet my son, Hercules," said Zooey.

Aphrodite?!

"Hercules, meet your half-sister, Aphrodite, goddess of beauty."

Another of the twelve Greek gods! Pav would be **sick** with envy.

"What we doing you for then?" asked Aphrodite, striding over and massaging my head like a hairdresser.

"I want to be the **coolest kid in school!**" I replied.

Aphrodite looked at Zeus and he nodded. She drew a long breath. "Gonna take some doing," she finally said. "But nothing's impossible..."

"You can't eat your own mouth," I replied, but she wasn't listening.

"What I'm thinking is we make these muscles twice the size..."

I nodded eagerly.

"We whiten his teeth. Give him a new haircut. Sculpt his eyebrows. Plump up these lips. Give him a spray tan. And get the coolest trainers and clothes on him. He'll look **great**."

I nodded so much my neck hurt. "And make me really sporty! Cool kids are **always** really good at sport. And really good at guitar."

"Well, that's not my..." she began, but was cut off by Zeus shouting into the air.

"Hermes! Apollo! Come here!" Then he dropped down into the chair next to me. "Better settle in. This is going to be a long afternoon."

My life is the absolute **best**. Over the next hour, I didn't just meet one Greek god but **three**! Each of them helped turn me from my old rubbish self to **Hercules Braver 2.0.**

HERMES
God of athletics (and messages, dreams and travellers).

Made me super sporty.

APHRODITE
Goddess of beauty.

Made me look super cool.

APOLLO
God of music (and medicine and shepherds).

Made me a sick guitarist.

When they were finished, I almost didn't recognize myself. I looked cooler, stronger, all-round more awesome. Finally, I look as **epic** as I knew I could.

When I got home, I rushed upstairs with my cardboard-box cat cage and shut Daphne in my bedroom. When I came down, all Mum and Ken could do was stare at me.

Finally, Mum said, "Have you had a haircut? And are those new clothes?" I shrugged and played it cool.

"I think you look rad, dude," said Ken, giving me a cheesy thumbs up. When he went to carry on fiddling with his coin-sorting machine, Mum turned to me and said, "What has Zooey done? What do you know about him?"

I looked as innocent as I could. "Nothing. He just treated me to a cool makeover."

She stared at me long and hard. "I think I'm going to need to speak with Zooey about this."

Then I remembered my deal with him. "Well, he wants to go for a coffee with you, actually!"

"Fine. When?"

"Tomorrow evening?"

"Done." Then she looked around. "Did you just hear a cat?"

"Nope," I lied, hurrying off to my bedroom as she narrowed her eyes suspiciously.

"Something's going on!" she shouted up the stairs after me. **"And I'm going to find out what!"**

But there's no way she will - because I'm **great** at keeping secrets.

Then I climbed into bed, gave fake-Daphne a little stroke in the box-bed I'd made her, and prepared for what was going to be **the greatest day of my life,** when everyone will finally realize how **awesome** I am.

THURSDAY
21 SEPTEMBER

When I walked into the school playground this morning, carrying a box with Daphne inside, everyone was gathered around the pond. They stared at its crystal-clear waters. An otter bathed lazily on its back and a kingfisher swooped down to perch on a reed.

Everyone was muttering things like "Who did this?" and "How?"

"It was me!" I announced.

Everyone turned, fell silent and stared at my new look. I shot them a finger pistol and I saw a couple of girls mouth, **"Wow."**

Hatty and Pav hurried over to me. "*You* did this? **How?**" asked Pav.

"Herc," said Hatty, "you look different. *Really* different. FasTek trainers? They're about seven hundred pounds. How did *you* afford *them*? And that jacket? And that bag?"

I didn't answer. Because it was time to bring out my ace card.

"Sir!" I called to Mr Geras, who was marvelling at the pond in confusion. "I believe I have something of yours." He turned, and I scooped Daphne from her box and held her up.

Mr Geras looked momentarily like he might faint. Then he leapt forward, grabbed her and hugged her tight.

"You found her! How?"

I flashed him a wink. "Magic!"

There was a pause, and then **everyone** laughed. Even Mr Geras!

"Hercules Braver!" He chuckled, holding Daphne to his cheek and showering her with kisses. "I had you all wrong. You are a **hero!**"

And with that, the whole school broke into applause, and a feeling warmer than a mug of hot chocolate flowed through me.

At last: they think I'm **awesome**. And it feels **incredible**.

First chance they got, Hatty and Pav grabbed me and dragged me into a quiet corner.

"Why do you look **SO** different?" asked Pav.

"Where did you find Daphne?" asked Hatty.

I wanted to tell them the truth **SO** badly. Instead, all I did was shrug. "I just found her near the pond." Which was a half-truth. Then I got out a Ribena and slurped it down in one. I dropped the carton on the floor, kicked it, and it arced over the heads of everyone and into a bin fifty metres away.

Pav was wide-eyed, shaking his head. "Do that again," he said, dropping his own juice carton on to the floor. I swung a leg at it, and it arced across the playground once again, landing cleanly into the bin. Everyone stopped what they were doing and clapped.

"Oh my days," said Hatty, stepping back and taking me in. "When did you suddenly get good at football? You used to be terrible."

Pav stared at me. I could see the cogs in his brain whirring, like he was trying to figure out some impossible sudoku. "Something's going o—"

But he was cut off by Billy, who was coming over with Ben. "That was amazing!"

"You've got some **skills!**" added Ben. "They're doing trials for the football team later. You should come along."

"Sure," I replied, shooting him a finger pistol. "And, hey, aren't you two in the school band?"

"We sure are," replied Billy.

"You need a new guitarist?"

"You don't play guitar," hissed Hatty.

"I do now," I whispered back.

"We sure do. Matthew's been auditioning for it since Malky left," said Ben (although I think he meant Natthew). "We're going to the music rooms now. You're welcome to audition as well?"

"Absolutely!" I replied. "Kalamata!" I turned to Hatty and Pav. "Wanna come?"

"Can you play an instrument?" Ben asked them.

They shook their heads.

"Sorry, then there isn't space," said Ben matter-of-factly.

"Oh," I said.

They both stared at me as Billy and Ben turned to leave.

"You coming?" asked Ben.

I hovered for a minute. There was a weird gurgling in my tummy. It might have been guilt, but I wasn't sure. Then I pushed it down and hurried after them, leaving Hatty and Pav by the bins.

Band practice was **awesome**. I did a ten-minute electric guitar solo and the rest of the band was so blown away that they made me lead guitarist instead of Natthew, who looked a bit sad about it. We've got our first gig this weekend.

Then I went to football trials and scored **fifteen** goals. They gave me the striker position, which is the position Malky used to play. Mr Geras shook my hand and said it was the first time a Year Seven has **ever** made the 1st team. Then he gave a big smile, patted me on the back and said if I carried on like this I'd be a school legend. Kalamata!

It was the **best feeling** in the world. At last – people can see how **amazing** I am!

When I got home, I was exhausted. Being cool is **hard work**. Downstairs, Ken was hovering. "Do you know where your mum is?" he asked.

"Nope," I said.

Then I realized I **did** know where she was. She was having that coffee with Zooey. Why hadn't she told Ken? I thought about it for a second, and something in me decided that he didn't need to know, so I kept quiet.

"I'm sure she'll be home soon," Ken said. Then he turned and went upstairs, and that weird gurgling feeling came back, although I'm not sure why.

FRIDAY
22 SEPTEMBER

I had another **incredible** day being **awesome.** At break time we had a football game, me vs everyone else. I won 20-0.

Pav and Hatty watched, although they didn't look as impressed as everyone else.

After school, Zooey picked me up. I high-fived everyone on the way to the car. Zooey seemed impressed by my new-found popularity.

"You seem much more like a true son of mine," he said.

Like a son of **Zeus!** What a compliment.

"Did your mother speak of our date last night?" he asked.

"Date?" I said, glancing at him, tummy gurgling again. "You mean your coffee?"

"Yes, our coffee. Did she mention anything else?" asked Zooey, chuckling to himself.

"Like what?"

Zooey smiled. "Oh, I don't know ... like **flying her across the sky in Helios's sun chariot so we might survey all that I hold dominion over.**"

I thought long and hard. I don't always listen to what Mum says, but I'm pretty sure she didn't mention towing a giant ball of fire across the sky last night. In fact, now I *think* about it, all she did was complain about Zooey and call him "vain" and "arrogant".

"Not really..."

Zooey looked cross. "What must I do to stop her being so angry with me?"

"Tell me about it!" I said. "She can be tough on me as well. She was cross with me for *ages* when I got stuck in a vending machine. Sometimes I wish I could magically stop her getting angry with me ever again."

"Yes..." said Zooey, frowning in thought. "Yes ... that could work."

Then I spotted Hatty and Pav waiting for their parents on the other side of the car park. I waved at them, but I don't think they saw. They were with Natthew, who was trying to make them laugh, as they both looked a bit glum.

"Do you still hang around with those people?" asked Zooey.

"Yeah! Although not so much the last couple of days," I

replied, which reminded me of something I'd been meaning to ask him. "I was thinking, would you mind if I told Hatty and Pav about you and my wishes? It's just, they're my best friends and I don't like keeping this secret from them."

Silence. I glanced over at Zooey. He was scowling, hard.

"I already told you: **never** reveal my true identity. To **anyone**." The temperature in the car dropped. "It is **our** secret. You and your mother are the only mortals who know the truth. And it **must** stay that way. **Do you understand me?**"

"Yup," I squeaked. I wished I'd never asked.

"I do not wish for humankind to remember I exist. They are hassle."

"OK."

The atmosphere had got awkward. I hadn't meant to annoy him. I waited for a bit, then asked tentatively, "Can we still do something awesome together? Like go and do some archery with Artemis? Or some athletics with Nike?"

Zooey cleared his throat. "I have things to do. Ruling the universe is not easy. I will drop you straight home."

"OK, sure," I said, my heart sinking.

The rest of the drive was quiet.

"Oh, son?" he said as we pulled up at home.

"Yes?" I replied hopefully.

"Tell your mother that I can't pick you up from school on Monday."

"Oh. OK," I said. "But we're still cool, aren't we?"

"Yes, we are still ... *cool*, my son." And then he flashed me a smile. Although his eyes didn't look as sparkly as they usually do.

All evening, I still felt a bit hurt that Zooey had got cross with me. Ken must have noticed, because he sat down next to me when I was watching TV and asked me if I was OK.

"Yeah, fine," I said.

Then he told me how it must be confusing having my birth dad back, and that I wasn't alone in feeling that.

I stared at him. Was he talking about him? Or Mum? Or both? I suddenly got a really strong urge to tell him everything. But I knew that would be a bad idea, so I just shrugged and said nothing.

SATURDAY
23 SEPTEMBER

I woke up this morning feeling a lot happier. Having slept on it, I realized that of **course** Zooey would have been cross with me for wanting to reveal his true identity. It would be **SO** annoying to have everyone begging him for wishes and to fix all their problems. That was just reserved for **special** people like me.

Normally either Hatty or Pav or both would pop round on a Saturday, but neither of them did today. I didn't really notice until it got late into the evening, as I was so busy texting with Billy and Ben about our new band and what songs we could play. Being cool involves a lot more admin. But is a **lot** more **fun**.

MONDAY
25 SEPTEMBER

At school, there was an unexpected visitor. I was busy showing off how I can do over a thousand keepy-uppies, when who should walk in but this guy...

Apparently, he is staying with his aunt but will be moving back in three weeks and was just dropping in today to pick up some homework.

He saw me and scowled, hard. "Why's everyone

watching *this* **loser**?"

"He's the new striker for the first team," said Billy.

"Yeah!"

"But **I'm** the striker for the first team," spat Malky.

Once upon a time I would have been scared of him, but not now I am extra-**awesome**.

"No, **I am**," I replied. "Because I'm better and stronger and faster."

He looked like he might explode with rage.

"No you are **not!**"

"**Prove** it!" I said, suddenly feeling emboldened to stand up to him. "Try and beat me in a race."

He snarled. "Easy. When?"

"After school," I said.

"I'm going back to my aunt's as soon as I've picked up my homework. Make it my first day back."

"When's that?"

"Three weeks' time. Tuesday seventeenth of October - Mr

Geras says I have to be back by the day of the science fair by the latest."

"Done!"

"Winner is the striker for the rest of the season," said Malky.

"Fine," I replied. But I didn't just want to beat him. I wanted to humiliate him. "And ... the loser has to do a lap of the sports field in their underwear shouting 'I'm a loser! I'm a loser! I sniff Mr Geras's pants'."

"Whoooooaaaahhh!" said the crowd.

"Fine. Deal," he laughed. "I can't wait to beat you, loser!"

"Whhhhhhhhhooooooaaaa!" repeated the crowd, as Malky stomped inside.

It was hotting up. But I'd never been so sure of anything in my life: I was going to trounce Malky. I turned away, feeling smug.

In the crowd, I saw the faces of Hatty and Pav. They just

stared at me, like they didn't understand what I had just done or even who I was. I tried to go over and chat to them, but everyone else crowded around me to say how awesome I was for standing up to Malky. And when the bell finally rang for class, Hatty and Pav had gone.

After school, I had to wait aaaaaages for Mum to pick me up. I could have just walked home, but she doesn't let me unless I'm with someone else, and Hatty and Pav left without me. When she did finally pull into the car park, I was the only kid left. She got out of the car, flustered and apologetic. I was about to climb in, when I heard the roar of an unmistakable engine: Zooey's gold sports car swung around the corner.

"What the...?" said Mum. "But he said he couldn't..."

Zooey screeched to a halt. And I could have **sworn** I glimpsed someone next to him in the passenger seat - a little pudgy face with curly blonde hair.

Zooey climbed out and looked at Mum like he was surprised to see her. "What? I thought *I* was doing pick-up," he said, smiling.

That's definitely not what he said on Friday.

Mum folded her arms. "No, you said..."

Zooey hit his palm against his forehead. "Forgetful me! I have muddled up my days." He was smirking ever so slightly.

I glanced back at his car, but the little face had gone.

Mum narrowed her eyes. "You are up to something, Zooey. I *know it*. And whatever it is, I'm going to get to the bottom..."

"Ow!" screamed Mum, clutching her bum. "Something bit me! Something bit me on the bottom!"

She hopped up and down. "What is it? What is it?"

I looked and there was a little gold pin stuck in her bum. "You must have sat on something, Mum," I said, pulling it out and showing it to her, before slipping it into my pocket.

She winced again. "That *really* hurt."

Weirdly, Zooey's smirk had got bigger. And that's when I

swear I saw the podgy little face again, peering out of some bushes at the side of the car park.

"Come on, Herc," said Mum. "If Zooey really wanted to collect you, he should have confirmed plans earlier."

And with that, we drove off. Although I was a bit sad I couldn't hang out with Zooey again.

TUESDAY
26 SEPTEMBER

Mum has the flu. She said she felt **weird** as soon as she got home last night. Then she just sat and stared at the wall while Ken and I watched TV. This morning, she said she wanted to stay in bed, and just stared at the ceiling. She doesn't seem to have a cough or a sniffle. She looks more like she's thinking really, really hard about something.

I probably don't need to worry about catching the flu. I imagine bad stuff like that doesn't happen to **demi-gods**.

FRIDAY
29 SEPTEMBER

I've been so busy being awesome, I've barely had time to write in here. I haven't seen Pav and Hatty properly for days either. Not since my mega makeover. Even though it's great being super popular, I miss hanging out with them.

I spotted them at break chatting with Natthew. I hurried over.

"Hi, guys!" I said.

"Oh, you've remembered us?" said Hatty, folding her arms.

They both seemed a bit frosty. "How come you are suddenly so ... **different** lately?" asked Pav.

"I'm not," I said, brushing some dirt off my new trainers. "I'm still the same old Hercules."

"Except you are **suddenly** good at football, and can

196

play the guitar, and think you can beat Malky in a race when you are the slowest person I've ever met," said Pav. "*And* you don't hang out with us any more."

"I liked you just as much before!" said Natthew, smiling at me.

"Yeah!" said Hatty, narrowing her eyes. "What's happened? You've **changed** since your birth dad turned up."

I wanted to tell them **so** badly. But I knew I couldn't. So I just said, "I've got cooler, that's what's happened - just like I said I would." Then I added, "And you guys are cooler as a result." Though they were on their own by the bins, so I realized that wasn't *necessarily* true.

"It's just all so unbelievable..." said Pav.

"I know!" I replied. "It is **unbelievable** how popular I am now!"

"No. As in, I **don't believe** that you've suddenly just got good at guitar and football. Something is going on."

"It's **almost** like you got granted some wishes by Zeus

or something!" said Hatty, snorting at how preposterous it seemed.

I pretended to laugh along.

Natthew chuckled. Pav laughed too – a short, knowing laugh.

HA! HAHAHAH AHAHHAHAHA HAHAHAHA!

"You'd better **hope** not! If Zeus had granted you wishes, then he would almost certainly want something in return. He's **sneaky**."

Obviously he doesn't know *my* Zeus. All he wanted was to go for a coffee with my mum. What could be sneaky about that?

When they stopped laughing, Pav said, "So what **is** going on?"

"And why have you forgotten that we exist?" said Hatty.

"Nothing's going on!" I said. "And I haven't forgotten you exist. I was coming over to say let's hang out tomorrow. We could walk Rocky III in the park?"

"Great!" said Natthew. I wasn't actually talking to him, but he could tag along if he wanted.

Hatty and Pav both stared at me warily.

"Fine, OK," said Pav, although I could tell he still thought something fishy was going on.

He was interrupted by Billy, who bowled up and said, "You ready for the big match tomorrow afternoon, Herc?"

Argh! The big match! I'd completely forgotten. I looked at Hatty and Pav, who stared at me, willing me to choose them over the football team.

"Come on, dude!" said Billy. "We need you. You're our star striker!"

He was right – I couldn't let him down. "Why don't we walk Rocky III on Sunday?"

Hatty looked away. Pav huffed.

"Whatever," said Hatty.

I felt so bad. Billy started to drag me away to do some shooting practice. "Sunday!" I called.

When we'd got a bit of a distance away, Billy said, "Good choice. Why are you still hanging out with those losers anyway?"

I glanced over my shoulder to see if they'd heard. And I felt that weird gurgle in my tummy because I'm pretty sure they did.

The football team had its big match. We won 30-0. I scored **all** the goals. At the end, the whole team lifted me up and gave me the bumps.

Kalamata!

Afterwards, we went for burgers. All the football team called me an **animal** for scoring so many goals. But they didn't specify which one. They probably meant a lion. Or a T-Rex.

I sat there listening to them talking about their favourite football teams again, and I realized that I would have loved Hatty and Pav to be there. I even missed Pav being grumpy. It's great how awesome the football team thinks I am, but if I'm completely honest, they are a *little bit* boring. I wish we could *all* hang out together, so that I could feel awesome, but I could be with Hatty and Pav too. But that wasn't going to ever happen as Billy and Ben and co. all thought they were losers.

And that's when I realized: I still had my **final wish** from Zooey! And I knew **exactly** what I could use it for.

When I got home, I was buzzing about making my last wish. Ken was on his own, still trying to get his coin machine working. The lid kept malfunctioning and closing so tight he couldn't open it again without taking the whole thing apart.

"Where's Mum?" I asked.

"She's out."

He looked like he had something on his mind. "Where?"

"She's, um, out with Zooey."

"Oh." Maybe she was telling him off for getting the school pick-up dates mixed up on Monday?

Then he asked, a bit cagily, "Has she been talking to you about Zooey?"

"Nope," I said. "What's she been saying?"

"Oh, you know ... nothing important," he said, but he didn't seem himself.

Poor Ken. It must be hard for him watching Mum hang out with an ex-boyfriend. Feeling particularly awesome, I decided I'd do what any good person would do: I'd have a quiet word with Zooey to be mindful of Ken's feelings.

Sometimes, I surprise myself with how thoughtful and perceptive I can be.

SUNDAY
1 OCTOBER

I asked Zooey if he could meet me in the park today. It couldn't wait until tomorrow – I had something so important to ask.

"I want to use my **last wish!**" I said, as we sat down on the bench from which he'd lightning-bolted Malky's house.

He yawned, rubbed his eyes and said, "What is it that you wish for, my son?"

"I want my friends Hatty and Pav to be **awesome**, just like me!" I was so excited just thinking how pumped Pav would be when he got a **Greek god makeover.**

Zooey massaged his temples. "Fine. Is this what you really want?"

I nodded eagerly.

"Now?"

"Y..." I started to say, and then it dawned on me that I should probably tell them first. They would be **SO** happy. "Tomorrow."

"Fine, my son. Tell me when and I will make it so." Then he put his head in his hands. "In the name of Gaia, why does Dionysus punish me so!"

I asked the obvious:

Who's Dionysus?

"A half-brother of yours. The god of wine. Your mother and I did partake of his bounty last night."

"You did what?"

"We drank a lot of wine together."

So *that's* what they were doing. Weird, considering Mum doesn't even like Zooey. I thought of Ken too, sitting on his own and nervously tinkering with his coin-sorting machine, and thought maybe I should say something.

"Um, do you think you could maybe *not* hang out with Mum?"

Silence. I looked across at him and flinched.

"What did you say?"

I felt my head sink into my shoulders. "It's just ... um ... I think it made Ken sad, and..." I was already regretting it, because I could see one  of Zooey's moods coming on, and they are terrifying.

"Who do you think you are, telling me, the King of the Gods, what to do?"

"Um ... your son?" I mumbled.

"Ha! The least impressive of my sons dares to instruct me how to live my life? Dares to question an immortal god!"

A single storm cloud rolled into view. Then Zooey thrust his hand up at it, like he was Spider-Man casting a web, and I nearly jumped out of my skin as a lightning bolt burst down and exploded into a tree.

He drew in angry breaths with great heaves of his chest,

and finally he said, "**Never** dare to question me again."

I sat there, frozen rigid, scared and upset.

And all I could think was: but Mum doesn't even *like* you.

MONDAY
2 OCTOBER

Spent all yesterday evening thinking about how angry Zooey got again. But, after I'd slept on it, I realized everything was still going to be fine. OK, Zooey doesn't like being told what to do. But neither do I! And anyway, he was still going to grant my final wish, and that's pretty amazing, right?

When I arrived at school, the football team were doing what they usually do - chatting about their favourite goals and swapping football cards - and they tried to rope me in. But I needed to find Hatty and Pav - I had to tell them about my plan to make them cool. Then we could all hang out together.

Finally, I found them with about five minutes to spare before class started.

"Guys!" I shouted. "How would you both like to be as cool as me?" It came out sort of wrong, so it wasn't the best start.

Hatty folded her arms. Pav glowered at me.

"And just *how* do you propose to make us 'cool'?" asked Pav.

I'd thought about this. I wasn't *allowed* to tell them about Zooey, so I said, "Erm, this really special, uh ... salon my birth dad showed me."

Finally, Hatty said, "Hercules. We know. Pav worked it out."

"Know what?" I asked.

Pav stepped closer and lowered his voice. "That your birth dad is Zeus."

"I... I..." I was lost for words. Part of me was over the moon that they finally knew. The other half was terrified because I wasn't supposed to let on about Zooey's real identity.

"It was all so *suspicious* – Malky's house being destroyed

by lightning, the pond, Daphne, your sudden coolness. It **was** magic."

I stared at him. I should've known this wouldn't get past Pav. He might be grumpy, but he has a brain the size of a cow.

"We were walking Rocky III in the park yesterday, just like you asked us to … remember?" said Hatty.

I winced. I'd completely forgotten we'd arranged that. I'd stood them up!

"We were about to go home when we saw you on a bench with Zooey. He looked really, really cross, so we didn't come near. And then he did the weirdest thing…"

I knew what was coming next…

"He summoned a lightning bolt," continued Pav. "**A lightning bolt!**"

"*Who does that?*" asked Hatty.

"I'll tell you who," said Pav. "**Zeus.**"

I didn't say anything. I *couldn't* say anything.

"It's almost unbelievable, but there is **no other**

explanation!" continued Pav. "**Zeus is real**. He's alive. He's back … and … and *he's your dad.*"

There was no point denying it. I had to come clean.

"**OK!** Fine! I admit it! Zooey is really Zeus," I said, then the biggest smile of relief broke out over my face. "How **awesome** is that?! You must be so pumped, Pav! It's all real - the **Greek gods are real!**"

Pav didn't looked pumped. He looked the opposite of pumped. He looked edgy, anxious. "You don't understand, Herc. The Greek gods are **complicated**. You can't trust them. They can give, but they can also take away. They are sneaky, selfish, vindictive…"

Urgh. Pav. *Always* glass half-empty. "How can you be down on this? Zooey gave me *wishes!*" I argued. "Four wishes. I wished for the pond to be cleared. I wished that Daphne would come back. I wished to be cool. Now I want to use the last one on you guys … to make you **cool too!**"

Silence. They both stared at me. I was expecting something like this:

Instead, I got this:

What?!

"But I can make you **popular**! Just like **me**! Then we can all hang out with the cool kids together!" I said.

"But we don't want to hang out with them," said Hatty blankly.

"We don't *want* to be cool," repeated Pav.

That was the most ridiculous thing I'd *ever heard*. Who doesn't want to be cool?

"It's not real," said Hatty, gesturing at me. "None of this is real. It's not *you*. And I want to be ... me."

I was flabbergasted. I had to make them see sense. "But, guys, this is what we've always wanted!"

"It's what **you've** always wanted," said Pav.

I glanced over at the football team, then back to Hatty and Pav. "But ... but... They think you're..." And before I could stop myself, the word just fell out of my mouth. "*Losers.*"

The hurt was written all over their faces. I screwed my eyes shut. I shouldn't have said it. I tried to dig myself out. "But you're not! It's just what *they* think."

The bell rang. Hatty linked her arm through Pav's.

213

"Come on, Pav," she said. "He won't want to hang around with losers like us."

And like that, they marched off, leaving me standing there alone, the guilt cramping my tummy.

The rest of school was a drag. All I could think of was how cross Hatty and Pav were with me.

We played a training match at football practice. My heart wasn't really in it, so I only scored ten goals. Afterwards, the football team all talked about an amazing goal someone or other scored, but it was so boring I stopped listening. Why were Hatty and Pav so stubborn? If they'd accepted the wish, we could be here hanging out together **and** being cool.

I waited in the car park for Zooey to pick me up, but he didn't. I don't know if he'd forgotten or he was busy ruling the world or something, but I had to walk home on my own.

When I got home, I was still feeling sad. I found Ken at the kitchen table. He was holding a cup of tea in both hands and staring blankly at the wall. I threw my bag on a chair.

"Where's Mum?"

"Upstairs," he said, still staring at the wall. "She's got something she wants to tell you."

I moped upstairs, ready to unload on her how being the most popular kid in the history of the school is no walk in the park.

But the minute I stepped into her bedroom, that problem popped like a pricked balloon. Mum was leaning over her bed, hurriedly stuffing clothes in her bag.

"What are you doing?" I didn't understand. Were we going on holiday?

She looked at me, her eyes red like she'd been crying. "I've got to leave, Herc."

I still didn't understand. "Are you going on a work trip?"

"No. I'm going to stay with Zooey."

"Oh." That didn't make sense. She didn't *like* Zooey. "Why?"

"Because...." She paused and took a breath to steady herself. "I've realized ... I'm still in love with him."

What?! I did not see **that** coming. My head spun. I thought of what she said after their coffee "date", when she'd called him vain and arrogant. "But ... I didn't think you liked him?"

"I didn't when he first came back. But the last few days a lot of my old feelings - from twelve years ago - have come back. I didn't expect it at all. But I can't hide from them any more."

I was reeling. Mum and Zooey? Was that a bad thing? I did **want** a cooler dad... Then the realizations began to fall like dominoes. Where would I live? What would happen to our house? And **what** would happen to Ken? I couldn't get over the image of him sitting there, staring into space. He must be **devastated**. We're the only family he's got.

Mum picked up her suitcase and heaved it down the stairs in a hurry. I followed, my head still spinning. I hadn't expected *this* to happen when I wrote to Zooey. And when I saw Ken still sitting in the kitchen in a stunned silence, I couldn't help wondering if this was all my fault.

Mum stared at Ken. She called at him down the corridor, her voice wavering, "I'm sorry. So sorry."

Ken looked up with sad puppy-dog eyes. All he did was nod.

Mum fixed me in her gaze, trying not to cry. "I'm going to stay with Zooey for a bit. You can stay here with Ken. Or you can come with Zooey and me."

"I... I..."

Go with Mum and my birth dad, Zeus, King of the Gods? Or remain here with Ken and his sadness and his inventions? I looked at him, sitting there still holding his cold cup of tea, not arguing or fighting or getting angry or throwing lightning bolts. I didn't know what to do, what to say...

Then Ken said to Mum, "I've left twenty pounds by the front door for you to get a taxi. It's not safe to drive like this."

That was Ken - always thinking of other people. And I realized it *was* all my fault. If I had never written to Zooey, **none** of this would ever have happened, and Ken wouldn't be heartbroken.

"I'm going to stay," I said.

Mum's bottom lip quivered. She stroked my cheek. Then she turned and left, leaving a big hole where ten minutes ago our family had been.

FRIDAY
6 OCTOBER

I haven't really felt like writing in my diary. Everything has turned from gold into rubbish. Mum is gone, Zooey won't answer my texts and Hatty and Pav are ignoring me.

I just drift through the days at school, being awesome but feeling awful. At home, Ken and I just mostly sit in silence and watch TV. Well, I watch TV. He just stares out the window. Every now and then he'll ask if I'm OK, while still looking out the window. I've never seen him like this. He was always the cheerful one. Now, he looks like he's had the life sucked out of him.

I can't believe Mum just left like that. It doesn't feel real. And I can't **believe** how quickly she seemed to fall back in love with Zooey. It was weird. Out of the blue. Almost like it happened overnight.

What's going to happen to Ken? Where will he live? I know he's desperately uncool and calls me Herky-Werky and takes me on freezing fishing trips, but he **is** my dad.

Tonight, he excused himself earlier than usual and said he was going upstairs to work on his coin-sorting machine. I thought I'd better offer to help, so I followed him up, only to be met with the sight of the lid snapping shut and coins flying across the room like shrapnel.

"Whoa!" I said, ducking as a pound coin whistled past my ear.

Ken stared at it for a second and then kicked the machine as hard as he could. Then - for the first time ever in front of me - he swore! I was shocked. And I think he noticed as he hung his head and mumbled, "Everything is broken, Herc. Everything."

Poor Ken. I didn't know what to say, so I got down on my hands and my knees and started picking the coins up off the floor. Silently, he crouched down and joined me, reaching under the chest of drawers for a coin. But instead, he pulled out a shoebox.

"I wondered where these had got to," he said, sitting down on the floor and opening the box. Inside were photos of Ken, Mum and - by the looks of it - me when I was much, much younger.

"I printed these out a few years ago so we'd never lose them!" He picked up a photo of him pushing me on a swing.

I reached in and pulled a handful out. I leafed through one by one: there was us at the zoo in front of some zebras, us at the funfair holding a big teddy, me riding my first bike with Ken pushing from behind. In every single photo, from the ones showing a baby in nappies up to my last day at primary school, there was Ken. Not Zooey - Ken.

He looked in his shoebox again and said, "I haven't had one of these for ages." Then he pulled out a little bag of colourful disc-shaped sweets.

"What is *that*?"

"It's a Flying Saucer," he said. "Here, try it."

It looked weird - not like the kind of thing you'd eat - but I popped it in my mouth to make him happy. The outer shell started to dissolve on my tongue.

"I used to give you one of these as a treat when you were four years old. I'd drop you off at nursery every day, but you always cried when you had to get out of the car. So we had a little deal - a Flying Saucer. It would always cheer you up. Our little secret."

Suddenly, as the shell melted away and a burst of fizzy sherbet tingled over my whole tongue, that memory surfaced, hazy and broken. Me in the back seat of his car, the fizzy-sweet flavour, feeling sad and happy, not wanting to leave Ken. It's weird what you forget, even when your memory is as amazing as mine.

"Do you know what **else** used to cheer you up?"

"Cash?"

"No." A flicker of that cheerful smile returned as he picked up my palm and traced a little circle in it. "Round and round the garden, like a teddy bear..." Then he walked his fingers up my arm. I knew what was going on. I let him do it because he seemed to be enjoying it. "One step. Two step..." I braced myself. **"Tickly under there!"**

I squirmed and laughed. It all came flooding back - the feeling of Ken cheering me up, like he always did. "Stop it!" I cried. Then I swallowed the last of the sherbet. "Do it again."

We both laughed. When we fell silent, Ken said, "You'll come visit me, won't you, if you go and live with Mum and Zooey?"

Suddenly, I felt crushed - more crushed than I thought was possible with my newfound coolness.

And that's when I made a vow: I **have** to talk to Mum and Zooey and sort this mess out. For Ken. For me. For our little family.

SATURDAY
7 OCTOBER

I texted Mum to ask if we could meet up - so I could convince her to come home. She sent me the address of a fancy spa at the edge of town.

I found her lounging by a swimming pool with Zooey, both kitted out in white bathrobes, sipping cocktails.

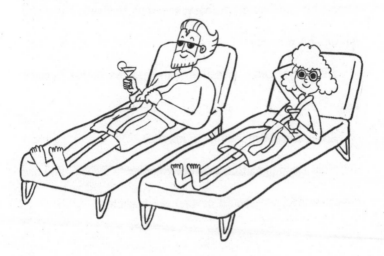

"Herc! You're here! I'm so glad you've changed your mind!" cried Mum, waving at me.

What was she talking about? "Changed my mind about what?"

"About coming to stay with us! Zooey booked the suite in the hotel here. It's amazing. There's a jacuzzi bath. Gold urns. Columns. Zooey **loves** gold urns and columns," she said. "And there's a room for you!"

Zooey just grinned, but my tummy was flitting with nerves over what I was about to say. If there is one thing I know for **sure** about Zooey, it's that he doesn't like not getting his own way.

"I'm not staying," I replied. "I'm here to ask you to come home."

Zooey's grin dropped from his face.

Mum seemed sad. "But I told you, Herc - Zooey and I are together now. We should never have broken up in the first place."

"And you should never have married that *loser*, Ken," muttered Zooey.

That made my blood boil. I am allowed to call Ken a loser. That's because he is my loser.

I tried to stay calm. "I know I wrote in my letter that I wanted to meet you, Zooey. But I didn't want you to break up Mum and Ken."

Zooey ignored me. It was like I hadn't spoken.

"So can you just come home, Mum?"

Zooey finally turned his eyes to me, and I felt like a tiny ant in his glare.

A masseuse quietly appeared by Mum's lounger and said in a hushed voice: "Are you ready for your massage appointment, Mrs Braver?"

Mum rose up, laying a pacifying hand on Zooey's arm. "This is our future, Herc, please don't fight it. Grab a drink – whatever you want, Zooey is paying." Then she lowered her voice to a whisper. "I know you know. He's the **King of the Gods**, you're his **son** and we're a **family** again – how **amazing** is that?" Then she stared adoringly at Zooey, planted a kiss on his lips (bleurgh) and walked off, leaving me standing there with rising panic in my chest.

I couldn't understand how Mum seemed to have suddenly fallen back in love with Zooey. Or why she was acting like everything was fine, when this was hurting Ken so much – and hurting me. Something didn't add up.

"You could have any woman in the world," I said to Zooey nervously. "Why Mum?"

Zooey locked me in his gaze and shrugged, coldly. "Unfinished business. I **always** get what I want. No one turns Zeus down."

"When did she turn you down?" I asked.

"Twelve years ago."

"Was that when she was pregnant with me?"

Zooey nodded. Gosh. That was some grudge.

Then a thought landed in my head with a horrible, jangling clatter. "Is that why you really came back? For Mum? Rather than for me? Were you hanging out with me ... *just to impress Mum?*"

Zooey didn't answer. His silence ripped my heart out and dropped it on the tiled floor.

Finally, I managed to say, "But she didn't even *like* you."

Zooey shrugged. "*Anyone* can be made to like *anyone*, if you know the right people." Then he smirked to himself. "Let's just say I had help from a little friend."

A little friend? Who was he talking about? Poseidon? Aphrodite? Or ... what about that little face I was sure I'd seen in his car?

Suddenly, it all started to add up. I reached into my pocket and rummaged. Was it still there? Yes - tucked in the corner was the pin that had been stuck in Mum's bottom that day. I pulled it out and held it close to my eye. Sure enough, just as I suspected, it was the shape of a tiny gold arrow!

"You had Eros shoot Mum with a love arrow!"

"I told you. I **always** get what I want." I felt myself dissolve in his fiery gaze. "Now get out of here," he snapped. "Before I do something I might regret."

And that's exactly what I did – I ran and didn't stop until I got home.

SUNDAY
8 OCTOBER

Mum is completely under Eros's love spell. I texted her last night to tell her the truth, but she doesn't believe me! I need to find another way to break Eros's spell.

I spent all of last night googling how you can undo his gold love arrow. Apparently, he needs to shoot Mum with a lead arrow to make her fall out of love with Zooey. But how can I ask Eros to help me without going through Zooey? I'm at a **complete** loss.

There was only one person in the world who would know what to do. One person who knew Zeus better than he knew himself: **Pav**.

I knocked on his door, and he and Hatty opened it.

"Thought you'd be hanging out with your *football friends*," said Pav.

"And calling us losers," said Hatty.

I felt bad all over again about that - the cherry on top of my massive pile of guilt and problems.

"Guys, I'm so sorry," I said. "Everything's gone wrong. I wish Zooey had never turned up."

Pav narrowed his eyes at me. I could tell there was an "I-told-you-so" lurking in there, but he didn't say it. "What's he done?"

I told them all about Eros's arrow and Mum leaving home and everything turning into poo.

Pav's scowl briefly wavered.

Hatty wasn't so forgiving. "Why don't you ask your *football friends* to help?" Then she tried to close the door on me, but I pushed it back open.

"**Please!** You have to tell me what to do!"

"If you had listened to me, I **warned** you about this," said Pav. "Yes, Zeus is all-powerful and all-mighty, but he's also **selfish** and **vindictive**."

"How can I fix things?"

Hatty started closing the door again.

Pav stuck his face in the closing gap and said, "Just remember what happened to Semele."

I tried to push back, but Hatty pushed harder. "What do you mean?"

The door slammed shut. I stood there trying to make sense of it. *What happened to Semele? Semele* had got burnt to a crisp!

"*That's* your advice?" I called through the door. "**Don't get burnt to a crisp?**" But he didn't answer.

FRIDAY
13 OCTOBER

I've been miserable all week. What's the point of being super-awesome if my friends **hate** me and my family has **split up**?

We had another football match at school. My heart wasn't really in it, but I still scored all the goals.

"How did you get so **good**, Braver?" asked Billy afterwards.

"My god dad granted me four wishes and I chose to be amazing at sport and super cool."

The team stared at me for a moment. And then they all broke out in laughter.

"**Good** one, Braver!"

"You're **SO** funny!"

In all honesty, I was beyond caring. Which, ironically, somehow made me **even cooler**.

After school, Mum rang to say she had something important to tell me. We met in the park. It was a bright, sunny, cold afternoon. She appeared in an expensive-looking coat. I gave her a little wave and she came down and sat next to me on the same bench I'd sat on with Zooey when he destroyed Malky's house and revealed his true identity.

That seemed like a **lifetime** ago.

"How's Ken?" she asked.

"Really sad."

"Mm," she said - a sort of guilty noise. "I didn't want to hurt him, you know. But Zooey and me, we have so much **history**."

"History is in the past," I said, but she carried on.

"When we first met, I was a young backpacker. He was this **mysterious, handsome** bar owner, and we fell in love. After a few months, he told me he was Zeus. I'd never felt so special in my whole life - the King of the Gods, in love with **me!** Then I found out I was pregnant with you. We were going to start a family together in Greece. But then, well ... Zooey can be pretty selfish. **Very** selfish. I couldn't stand him any more. So one morning, I snuck out and flew home. I sent a couple of photos when you were born, but I never heard from him again until he turned up on our doorstep."

"But he's *still* selfish! He only came back to try and get you back - not to see me!"

"That's *terrible*," she said, then gazed into the distance. "But **SO** romantic!"

Argh. Mum was blind with love.

"I told you, you're only feeling like this because Zeus got Eros to shoot you with a love arrow! He's tricked you!"

"**Rubbish!** I just realized how **amazing** Zooey really is. I know he can be moody and angry. But he can be merciful too. And he's powerful. **So** powerful."

Eros had **really** done a number on her. I needed to break the spell. "I know Ken isn't all-powerful like Zooey. And I know he's uncool and rides a tandem and isn't very tall and loves fishing … but he's kind and thoughtful and he loves us. He's my **dad**. My actual dad. The one who has been around for me since I was tiny!"

Mum was silent for ages. Thinking. For a hopeful second, I thought that maybe me pouring my heart out might have made her see sense, might even have undone Eros's arrow. But then she finally spoke and crushed all my hopes. "I really don't want to hurt Ken. But I can't ignore my feelings. He's a good man. I'll miss him. And I'm sure you will too."

I felt a sudden chill. "What do you mean?"

"This is what I came here to tell you - I'm moving to Greece with Zooey. We want you to come with us."

"What?!"

"He belongs in Greece - at Mount Olympus. I can't argue

with that. But he's going to get us a place nearby, where he can visit us."

No. No. No. No. Leave here? Leave Ken? Leave Hatty and Pav? I could hardly compute it all. I felt sick. There was no way in a million years I wanted to do that. But then the alternative was watching Mum leave. And I could never do **that**.

"I can't... You can't..." I mumbled.

"We can be a family at last! Think about that!"

Mum beamed like she was the **happiest** person in the world. There was no point trying to reason with her while that love arrow was working its wicked magic.

I wish I'd **never** written that letter. Because if I can't find an antidote to Eros's arrow, Mum will be moving to Greece and I'll either be saying goodbye to her, or goodbye to Ken. And both scenarios make me feel sick to the pit of my stomach.

SATURDAY
14 OCTOBER

I've been thinking long and hard about how I can sort out the mess I'm in and I've basically got three options.

1) **Beg** Zooey not to take Mum to Greece.

2) Use my last **wish** to ask Zooey not to take Mum to Greece.

3) Somehow **shoot Mum** with a lead arrow and hope that it breaks Eros's spell.

The first two are pretty much out. I've seen how Zooey reacts when I try to tell him what to do. He gets **really** angry. And the warning from Pav (who's still not speaking to me) is ringing in my ears:

Just remember what happened to Semele!

I **do not** want to get burnt to a crisp. It'd be **rubbish**.

I'm left with only one option: to shoot Mum with a lead arrow. I don't have a lead arrow, so I'm improvising and using this:

All I needed to do was make a bow with some string and a stick. After about thirty minutes' work, I was doing OK, I thought.

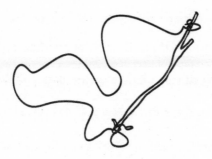

Ken came into my room and looked at it. "Is it a sculpture?"

"It's a bow."

"Ah. Can I?"

"Be my guest," I replied.

He sat down on my bed and began untangling it.

"So, you know that Mum is moving to Greece?" he said sadly, as he worked at a particularly tight knot.

I nodded. "Yeah. And she wants me to go with her."

He was silent for a bit. Then he said, "Whatever you want to do, I support you. It's your birth mum and birth dad. I completely understand if you all want to be a family." His voice wavered a bit, like he might cry. "I consider myself very lucky to have had the chance to get to know you these last eleven years."

He tied a final knot and handed me back a slightly better-looking bow.

"Don't worry," I said. "It's not going to come to that."

He gave a little frown. "How so?"

"Because I'm going to fix **everything** and get Mum back."

Then he looked at me and my bow and pencil arrow. And I could see he didn't believe me.

SUNDAY
15 OCTOBER

Today is the day I put my plan into action. I'm going to shoot Mum with my pencil and hope that it breaks Eros's spell. It's a **massive** long shot, but I don't have any better options.

I rang Mum and asked if we could meet.

I went to her fancy spa hotel suite and knocked on the door, my bow and arrow stuffed up my sleeve.

Zooey opened it in his robe. "My son," he said, looking smug. "You have chosen to come with us. A **wise decision**. My chariot flies this afternoon."

"Can I help Mum pack?" I asked, dodging an answer.

"Go ahead."

I tiptoed through Zooey's giant hotel suite, weaving

through urns and gold columns and into their room. Mum was packing clothes into a suitcase. She didn't notice me sneak in, but as I slipped the bow and arrow from my sleeve, her ears pricked and she turned around.

"You're coming with us!" She beamed. Then her eyes lowered to my bow and arrow.

Mum raised one eyebrow. "What are you doing?"

"Trust me, this is for your own good. Eros shot you with a gold arrow to make you fall in love with Zooey. Now I need to shoot you with a lead arrow to undo it."

"Herc, no one shot me with—"

I pulled the bow taut. She turned and covered her face and...

"Ow!" she said, rubbing her bum. "That hurt!"

I'd landed my shot! Now all I had to do was cross my fingers that it worked...

Zooey walked in. "What takes place in here?"

I watched Mum, every single finger and toe crossed that she would see Zooey and **instantly** dislike him once again.

She looked at him, staring deep into his face. She frowned, lost for words.

"Darling, what has taken place?" repeated Zooey, frowning now too.

"Mum...?" I said, the hope too much to bear.

She was looking between Zooey and me. "How dare you shoot me? How **dare** you?!"

Was she talking to me? Or Zooey? My heart was beating thump, thump, **thump**.

"Sometimes I really do wonder what goes on in your head!"

Go on, I silently begged. *Tell Zooey you hate him!*

"You can be so strange ... **Hercules Braver.**" Her eyes landed on me.

The hope rushed out of me like a burst dam.

"Just *what* was that about?"

I felt my shoulders slump. I knew it was a long shot, but I still felt crushed that it hadn't worked.

"I was trying to make you fall out of love with Zooey and come back home," I mumbled.

Mum's face was torn between sympathy and exasperation. "I *told* you, Herc. You need to accept that I'm with Zooey now."

Beside me, I could feel the anger **radiating** off Zooey. "How **dare** you try to undo the will of the gods!"

Thunder rumbled, and grey clouds poured in through the doors, hugging the ceiling like smoke. I'd **really** made him cross this time.

"Zooey, darling, please calm down," said Mum. "You have *such* a temper."

"I am **sick** and **tired** of this boy's insolence!" he shouted.

More thunder. I felt my knees shaking. But I was also angry.

I was **angry** at Zooey for pretending that he wanted to hang out with me.

I was **angry** at him for having Eros shoot Mum with a love arrow.

I was **angry** at him for wanting to take Mum back to Greece.

And – maybe most of all – I was **angry** at Zooey for upsetting Ken.

"Yeah, well, I'm sick and tired of **you**!" I shouted.

His face went beetroot with rage. Pav's words rang in my ears.

Remember what happened to Semele!

It looked like I was about to get burnt to a crisp.

Zooey roared, "Never have I been spoken to like this by any of my children, let alone the most pathet—"

"Stop it!" cried Mum, on the brink of tears. "Stop arguing with each other! You are family!"

"Pfffff, supposedly!" retorted Zooey. "But how could *he* be my flesh and blood? You are no **Greek god!** You look more like ... a **Greek yoghurt!**"

Zooey had finally shown his true colours, spinning out the

same insults as Malky.

Mum looked at me in distress, her eyes full of tears. It was almost like, deep inside, her love for me was battling Eros's poison – and *almost* winning, almost snapping her out of her trance. But that poison was just **SO** strong. I had to defeat it myself.

"Yeah?" I shouted. "Well, maybe I'd **prefer** to be a Greek yoghurt if being a Greek god means being like **you!** I **wish** you'd never turned up."

Even though I *did* still have one wish left, he wasn't even listening. But Zooey's so selfish I'd **never** expect him to grant a wish he didn't want to.

"Imagine a **puny, feeble mortal** like you trying to defy me!" he bellowed, picking up my bow and arrow. "And with what? These pathetic *sticks?*" He snapped them between his fingers.

Sticks. I'd heard that word before. And somehow, I instantly knew it was important. That it could help me.

Sticks.

Sticks.

Styx.

River Styx! Pav had talked about it. I screwed my eyes

closed and tried to remember why it was important.

If the gods swore an oath on the River Styx, they had to fulfil it or they would be chucked off Mount Olympus.

Suddenly, things started to fall into place. Pav's words

came rushing back: *"Remember what happened to Semele!"*

and I saw them in a new light. He wasn't warning me not to

get burnt to a crisp. He was telling me what to do! Zooey

swore an oath on the River Styx to grant me

four wishes! Just like he swore to Semele! That means he **has** to grant them! Whether he likes it or not!

There were more blasts of thunder.

I shouted over the noise. "I **wish** you would go away!"

Zooey didn't hear. He was still bellowing about how no one tells the gods what to do.

I yelled as hard as I could. "I *said*, 'I **wish** you'd go **away and that everything could go back to how it was before you arrived**'!"

This time, Zooey *did* hear.

"Come again?"

"I **wish** you'd go away and that everything could go back to how it was before you arrived."

There was a long, silent pause. Finally, with one eyebrow raised, Zooey said, "You *wish* this?"

"I **wish** it! And you **swore** on the River Styx to grant me four wishes."

His other eyebrow rose to meet the first. "Yes... Yes I did."

He had the surprised face of a chess grandmaster who'd just been checkmated by a rookie. "If I grant this, all your previous wishes will be undone. The pond, the cat, your popularity."

"Fine," I said. "I don't care." And when I thought about it, I genuinely didn't. I thought of me scoring all those goals, getting lifted up by the football team, jamming with the band. Then I thought of me walking Rocky III with Hatty and Pav. And I realized I was happier being plain old me. I didn't need all those special coolness powers. Ken was right: I just needed to be myself - Hercules Braver.

"So be it," said Zooey. The thunder stopped, the storm clouds disappeared, and a tiny smile curled in the corner of Zooey's lips. Maybe he was looking forward to going home. Or maybe, for the first time, it was a flicker of respect for me.

Mum looked back and forth from Zooey to me. "W-what's happening? What's going on?"

Zooey seemed strangely calm. I'll give him his dues - he could take being outsmarted. "Hercules Braver, I'm glad we met."

"I'm glad we met as well, Zooey."

"Here," he said, whipping out a bowl of black olives. "Have something to remember me by."

Goodbye olives

Then he shook my hand. "Goodbye, Hercules."

"Goodbye, Zooey."

Then he smiled and walked away. Just before he reached the door, he turned back and said, "I hope we will meet again one day."

There was a blinding flash, and I knew instinctively that Zooey - the King of the Gods, my biological father - had returned home.

I looked down at my shoes. My FasTek trainers and my cool jeans had gone, replaced by old tracksuit bottoms and tatty trainers. The wishes had been undone.

Mum stared at the door. "What ... just ... happened?"

I took a deep breath and said, "Zooey got Eros to shoot you with a love arrow so you'd fall in love with him." It was a sentence I'd *never* have imagined saying two months ago.

Now it was her turn to be livid. "That sneaky, selfish son of a..."

It had worked! Mum was **back!** I'd never felt more relieved about anything in my life. I flung my arms around her and hugged her tight.

"What about Ken?" said Mum, realizing what this meant. "He must be tearing his hair out!"

"Come on," I said, dragging her out. "We've got some explaining to do."

We *did* have some explaining to do. But we didn't tell Ken *everything*. There's no way he'd believe us. Mum just said that she'd made a terrible mistake and had come to her senses.

And Ken, being Ken, forgave her.

MONDAY
16 OCTOBER

Mum was back. Ken was happy. But there was still one thing I badly needed to fix.

I waited nervously at the start of school for Hatty and Pav to walk through the gates.

They laid eyes on me but kept walking.

"Please!" I cried after them. **"I'm sorry!"**

I fell on my knees and begged forgiveness. "I'm so sorry I called you losers! I'm so sorry I pretended I was too cool to hang out with you…"

Pav looked me up and down, then he glanced over at the pond. "Your clothes are rubbish again... And the pond is filthy... What's happened?"

"Zooey's gone!" I said. "I used my last wish. I wished for him to go home and for everything to go back to the way it was before he arrived, so we could be friends again!"

"He's *gone*?" said Pav.

"Gone. I listened to what you said about Semele," I replied.

That got a rare smile out of him.

"You wished away your coolness?" asked Hatty.

"Yup! I don't want to hang out with the football kids. I want to hang out with you two!"

"Aw," said Hatty, melting a bit.

"So *everything* is undone?" asked Pav.

I nodded. "The pond, Daphne, me. It's all just like it was before!"

Pav glanced over at the now-filthy pond. "But the teachers think vandals did that over the weekend..."

"So ... you're no longer super-fast and super-sporty?" asked Hatty.

I shook my head. "**Everything** is undone."

Her face fell. "But you have your race with Malky tomorrow!"

My *what*?! And then it all came flooding back. What with Zooey, Mum and Eros's arrow, I'd forgotten all about it. Malky would be back tomorrow and he was expecting to race me!

"You're going to lose," muttered Hatty. "And you're going to have to run around the field in your underwear shouting: '**I'm a loser! I'm a loser! I sniff Mr Geras's pants**'."

"Oh ... *farts*," I said. "Mr Geras will be **SO** upset and angry about Daphne being missing again too. He'll go **ballistic!** What am I going to do?"

Hatty pushed her mouth to the side. "We can't make you faster. And we can't smite Malky again. But we **can** find that cat. At least that would make him a tiny bit less likely to expel you?" She sounded more hopeful than certain. "We just desperately need some sort of trap. I'm **convinced** that's the way to get her!"

"But we've got no money and no one we know will lend us a pet cage..." said Pav.

We gazed out across the playground and into the car park. Ken was unloading his malfunctioning coin-sorting machine from his car, ready for tomorrow's science fair. As he placed it down on the floor, the lid sprung closed. He balled a fist at it in frustration, muttering complaints as he tried to prise it back open.

"What's that?" asked Hatty.

"It's Ken's really complicated invention for sorting coins," I replied.

"Is that lid motion controlled?" she asked, raising an eyebrow.

"I think so..."

She looked at the two of us. "I've got an idea."

For two hours after school, Ken, Hatty, Pav and me worked on turning the dodgy coin-sorting machine into something genuinely useful: a **cat trap**. Ken was only too happy because he was terrified of it being a laughing stock at tomorrow's Science Fair. Natthew came along as well, and it was useful having him about because every time we needed a spare part from the DT room, Natthew ran there and back at lightning speed. Plus, he was all right company. Even if he is still a bit desperate.

Thanks for inviting me!

"You're welcome, Natthew," I replied.

"His name's Matthew," said Hatty.

"It's not," I replied. "Is it, Natthew?"

He thought for a second, then said: "Actually, it is

Matthew. I just didn't want to make you look silly."

Oh.

"But I don't mind," he said. "It's just nice to have some friends to hang out with. You're a cool guy, Hercules."

Maybe it was the emotion of having Hatty and Pav back, but it tugged a heartstring.

"Thanks, Natthew," I replied. "And you're not nearly as rubbish as I first thought."

He smiled. He was probably choked up by the compliment.

"There!" said Ken, finishing the last bit of soldering. "Is that what you had in mind, Hatty?"

She walked around the coin-sorting machine. "It is exactly what I had in mind. The perfect cat trap."

It was a million times better than a malfunctioning coin-sorting machine.

"It's just like the pond monster trap!" said Matthew. "Do we use a Curly Wurly for bait?"

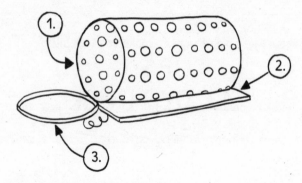

1. Bait goes here
2. Cat activates weight-detecting pad
3. Lid springs closed

"Cats don't like chocolate," replied Ken. "Any idea what food Daphne loves?"

I thought long and hard, right back to when I first let her out of her cage. And an idea went ping in my brain. "Olives! She loves olives!"

"Olives it is then!"

I tipped Zooey's bowl of goodbye olives into the trap, then we took it to the edge of the school field and set it. All we could do was wait and pray she was in it come tomorrow morning.

TUESDAY
17 OCTOBER

I woke up early, half excited to find poor Daphne, half terrified of racing Malky. At least getting the headmaster's cat back might *just* make him less angry when I have to run around the field shouting: **"I'm a loser! I'm a loser! I sniff Mr Geras's pants."**

Ken was up early as well, equally as excited to see if the trap had worked.

"Wanna go check now?" he asked.

He wheeled his tandem out, and I jumped on the back. As we cycled to school, he shouted over his shoulder, "I thought you might be too cool to ride on my tandem!"

Oh yeah! I hadn't thought twice about jumping on. We cycled past some of the football team, and I could see them sniggering. But I didn't care.

We pulled around the corner to where we'd left the trap and...

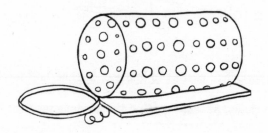

We both stared in disappointed silence. It was empty.

I waited by the trap for the next twenty minutes while everyone arrived, hoping - praying - that Daphne might suddenly show up before Malky did. But no luck.

"Oh," said Hatty, with a big sad frown. "Daphne didn't take the bait."

"No," I replied, as Malky swaggered through the gates. Everyone was talking yesterday about how the builders had rebuilt his house in record time (although I knew the truth - it was all thanks to my final wish, though I was hoping he'd forgotten about the footage...). But he clearly only had one thing on his mind.

"Oi, **Braver!** That copy of *Golden Deer Quest II* you gave me is **fake!** It stopped working the other day!"

Even uglier than
I remember

Then he said: "Boy, I'm going to **love** beating you in this race."

A crowd gathered around us.

"Race, race, race!"

I stared up into his sunken eyes. There was no way I could beat him. I looked at Hatty, Pav and Matthew for any ideas.

"Just say you can't do it!" whispered Pav.

No way. I'd made a bet. I intended to honour it.

"You can do it, Hercules! I believe in you." Matthew beamed, whipping out a double thumbs up at lightning speed.

And then something occurred to me: I **definitely** couldn't win. But I could also make sure that Malky didn't either...

"Matthew, why don't you race as well?"

He looked surprised. "Erm..."

"Trust me," I whispered. "I think you should race."

"I don't care who I beat!" bellowed Malky. "Let's just get on with it."

"Erm, OK," said Matthew.

"Losers run around the field in their underwear shouting, **'I'm a loser! I'm a loser! I sniff Mr Geras's pants',**" I said. "But winner gets to be **lead guitarist** for the school band."

"Fine, *whatever*," said Malky, so confident he would win that he didn't care what the stakes were. "Race to that tree."

Billy, Ben and the football team were all chanting my

name. I'd managed to avoid them all yesterday, so they had no idea how slow I now was. But they were about to find out.

We lined up in a row. The crowd counted us down.

"Three!"

"Two!"

I crouched down. I knew I wouldn't win. I just hoped that I'd got it right with Matthew.

"One!"

We all burst forward. I pumped my legs as hard as I could. My thighs ached. My lungs burned... And I was still in last place.

But out in front, Matthew was keeping up with Malky. In fact, he wasn't just keeping up with him - the weirdly fast little legend was streaking out in front! To look at Matthew, you'd think he'd be slower than a time-wasting tortoise. Malky

clearly did. And I guess it made me realize that there's loads more to all of us than how other people see us.

Matthew reached the tree at the finish line, and I collapsed on the ground, exhausted but delighted.

Then Malky leaned over me, his face puce with rage. "That's not fair! He wasn't supposed to race!"

"You agreed to it," I replied. "And remember what we said: *losers* have to run around the school field shouting..."

He lifted me up and thrust his face into mine. "You embarrassed me again! And now you're going to pay!"

I was **certain** he was going to hit me. But when I felt his hand grab the top of my boxers, I knew it was worse – he was going to wedgie me! If this was the price I had to pay for Malky not to win, then so be it. I shut my eyes and waited for the burning pain of fabric on bum crack.

But nothing happened. Nothing happened, because a single, high cry stopped everyone in their tracks.

Meow!

I peeked my eyes open. Everyone - even Malky - had frozen and was looking towards the bushes.

"Meow."

Someone shouted, "That's Daphne's cry!"

And suddenly, the whole crowd was rushing towards the sound. It was enough of a distraction for me to get free from Malky's grasp and run after them. Sure enough, there she was inside the cat trap!

Mr Geras was pushing his way through the crowd. "It's her! She's back again!" He saw the cat trap and beamed. "Who is responsible for this?"

I raised a hand. "Erm, we are, sir. Hatty, Pav, Matthew, me and my dad."

Ken came through the crowd and unscrewed the lid, allowing Mr Geras to pull Daphne from the cage, her mouth covered in greasy olive juice. He hugged her tight.

"You are all **heroes!**"

Suddenly, **everyone** clapped. It was a pretty cool

feeling, getting respect for something we'd achieved -
actually achieved, not had magically granted.

But just as I was basking in it, there was a feeling of
burning pain in my bottom.

Mr Geras's euphoria came crashing down to earth.

"Malky, what do you think you are doing?"

"He tricked me, sir! He went back on his word!"

Mr Geras began shouting at Malky, but I'd zoned it out.

Going back on my word is something I **never** do. And I was about to prove it.

I took my shorts and shirt off.

"What are you doing?" asked Hatty. "You're not going to ... are you?!"

"You don't have to do it!" cried Pav.

"Yes, I do," I replied. "If Zooey taught me one thing, it's that you have to honour your word. Malky and I both lost, which means we both have to do the forfeit we agreed. Care to join me?" I said to Malky, who scowled. Mr Geras broke off shouting at him to turn to me in surprise. But I'd earned myself this punishment, and now I needed to see it through.

And with that I set off around the playing field, gasps and laughter ringing in my ears.

I'm a loser! I'm a loser! I sniff Mr Geras's pants!

MONDAY
23 OCTOBER

Turns out everyone at school now knows the name Hercules Braver. I'm the kid who ran around the school playing field in his underwear shouting that he sniffed Mr Geras's pants. I suppose everyone's got to be known for *something*. Sure, it wasn't smiting a many-headed hydra or killing an unkillable lion, but it's an improvement on getting stuck in a vending machine or wearing a poo hat.

We are also the kids who found Daphne and won the Science Fair for inventing a cat trap. But Mr Geras didn't let me completely off the hook. He was still pretty angry about me running around the school field in my underwear. He gave me the same punishment as Malky. You guessed it: **Nature Club.**

But we weren't alone. Because these three volunteered to help out.

It's awesome hanging out with them again. Although Pav sometimes just stares at me and whispers, "I *still* can't believe you're the son of Zeus." But you know what? Being the son of a god didn't do me any favours. In fact, it made me appreciate how good I had it before Zooey even turned up: getting to hang out with Hatty and Pav every day, knowing Mum and Ken would be waiting for me at home. So even though Pav thinks it's pretty special, it's not. I'd rather be **Hercules Braver** than Hercules, son of Zeus.

Everyone in the school band agreed that Matthew should be the new lead guitarist as he won the race. His brother was so happy for him that he bought him this when it came out on Friday:

After every Nature Club, we go back to Matthew's house and play it. If you'd asked me two months ago how many new friends I'd have at school, I'd have said **one thousand**. Maybe even **one million**. But turns out I just have one: Matthew. But I'm fine with that. The other 999,999 will turn up when they're ready.

In a peace offering, we even asked Malky if he wanted to play *Golden Deer Quest II* with us. But he was practically sick when we suggested it.

"Why would I want to hang out with you **losers** any more

than I have to?" he said, pulling an old bin lid out of the mud while I scooped leaves out of the pond.

I don't know if she'd finally had enough of Malky, or she was just wanting to liven things up, but Hatty wasn't going to let him get away with that.

"Oh my days!" she cried. "It's the pond monster!"

Malky instinctively spun around, and Hatty pushed him as hard as he could. He staggered back into the pond until, with a splash and a high-pitched squeal, he disappeared under - before reappearing, looking wet, muddy and pathetic.

I reached out and dropped my net over his head. "There's your **pond monster!** And it's even more revolting than we imagined!"

We all laughed.

"Hercules, you're a hero!" said Matthew.

"... sort of," added Pav, with a wry smile.

And who am I to argue with that?

"Kalamata!"

Acknowledgements

My eternal thanks to:

Yasmin Morrissey and the team at Scholastic for the seed idea, and for so willingly going with me in the direction I took it. My brilliant editor Julia Sanderson for shepherding the book through many drafts; for a forensic eye for plot, character and detail; and for making the book the very best version of itself - I'm not sure I could have landed this one without you. David O'Connell for bringing Hercules, Zooey and co to life so incredibly, and for delivering all my silly little jokes better than I ever imagined. Sarah Baldwin for the amazing cover and design, and Claire Yeo for bringing everything together. Sarah Dutton and Jessica White for your copyediting and proofreading super-skills. The whole team at Scholastic - Lauren, Catherine et al - for your belief in me. My superstar agent Chloe Seager for making all of this happen, and for some creative masterstrokes when shaping the idea. The Year 4 classes at Upton Meadow, Farfield and Dormanstown primary schools for helping to name Mr Geras's cat - and Rosco at Dormanstown for the genius name of Daphne. And finally, a heap of love and thanks bigger than Mount Olympus itself to Issy, Albie and Agatha for making every day a laugh.

Other books by Tom Vaughan

A GANGSTER STOLE MY TRUNKS

TOM VAUGHAN

Illustrated by **NATHAN REED**

About Tom Vaughan

Tom Vaughan is a journalist, television producer, and children's author. Despite modest success in those three fields, he'd prefer to be remembered as the man who unsuccessfully tried to invent a meal between supper and breakfast called supfast. He lives in Yorkshire with his wife and two small unemployed people, also known as his children. *Hercules: the Diary of a (Sort of) Hero* is his third book after *Bin Boy* and *A Gangster Stole My Trunks*.